A CUT IN DIAMONDS

As Michael Kirk

A CUT IN DIAMONDS
MAYDAY FROM MÁLAGA
CARGO RISK
SALVAGE JOB
DRAGONSHIP
ALL OTHER PERILS

As Bill Knox

WAVECREST
THE HANGING TREE
BLOODTIDE
A KILLING IN ANTIQUES
BOMBSHIP
LIVE BAIT
WITCHROCK
PILOT ERROR
HELLSPOUT
RALLY TO KILL
WHITEWATER
DRAW BATONS!
STORMTIDE
TO KILL A WITCH
SEAFIRE
WHO SHOT THE BULL

BLUEBACK
THE TALLEYMAN
FIGUREHEAD
JUSTICE ON THE ROCKS
BLACKLIGHT
THE GHOST CAR
DEVILWEED
THE TASTE OF PROOF
THE SCAVENGERS
THE KILLING GAME
THE DRUM OF UNGARA
THE GREY SENTINELS
LITTLE DROPS OF BLOOD
IN AT THE KILL
LEAVE IT TO THE HANGMAN

As Noah Webster

AN INCIDENT IN ICELAND
A PAY-OFF IN SWITZERLAND
A WITCHDANCE IN BAVARIA
A BURIAL IN PORTUGAL
A KILLING IN MALTA
FLICKERING DEATH

A CUT IN DIAMONDS

MICHAEL KIRK

PUBLISHED FOR THE CRIME CLUB BY
DOUBLEDAY AND COMPANY, INC.
GARDEN CITY, NEW YORK
1986

M

All of the characters in this book
are fictitious, and any resemblance
to actual persons, living or dead
is purely coincidental.

Library of Congress Cataloging-in-Publication Data
Kirk, Michael, 1928–
A cut in diamonds.
I. Title.
PR6061.N6C8   1986   823′.914   85-20592
ISBN 0-385-23360-4

For Tony

"Another reason why BIMCO as an association takes a great interest in these matters is the wish to protect its members from being themselves the victims of maritime frauds.

"To this end, BIMCO will cooperate with any other association in an attempt to find out if there is an international gang of marauders behind cases of modern piracy . . ."

Spokesman, Baltic and International Maritime Conference, London.

A CUT IN DIAMONDS

PRELUDE

The small, grey-haired man was working at one hundred magnifications. Humming under his breath, concentrating totally on his task, he adjusted the tiny bead of back lighting a fraction of a degree and looked down at a frozen swirl of pale yellow mist. A miniature cosmos, it was marred by one harsh black blotch trapped far down within its depth.

The small, grey-haired man made a final note on the pad beside him.

The diamond was a seven-carat Light Cape, baguette cut in the standard sixty-two-facet pattern, an excellent stone totally ruined by that carbon inclusion. It had taken two painstaking hours to study the Light Cape, to be satisfied as to its structure and grain, to calculate its stresses.

Using a fine, specially tipped pen, he made one final tiny mark at an exact spot on the diamond's surface. Then he sat back.

The next stage would take only minutes. If he made the slightest error, there would be no second chance—the Light Cape would be ruined. But he seldom made errors, and success would increase the diamond's value several times over.

That was his art, his skill, developed over years which had begun when he was a young apprentice cutter, growing from there as he abandoned the orthodox and gradually, painstakingly created his own special techniques. He was a craftsman; the tiny diamond he wore inset in one thumbnail was a personal badge of pride.

After the Light Cape, he would take a break for an hour or so and indulge himself a little. There was another stone waiting, bigger, nearly ten carats, rose cut, showing all the basic sea-cold clarity of a top Blue Wesselton. But it was a relatively worthless reject, with a whole series of flaws clearly visible to the naked eye. They ranged from a coarse network of butterfly veins to what looked like a seed garnet imprisoned in its heart.

The seed garnet was deep red, the colour of blood. The smile faded from his lips; then he pushed the thought from his mind. He was well paid and had learned not to ask questions. He had no illusions about the nature of his employers, and they had told him another parcel of stones would arrive soon.

He would be busy again. Where the diamonds came from, how they were obtained, what happened to them afterwards were aspects he preferred to ignore.

Far better to consider the challenge of the flawed Blue Wesselton. It had been cut from the rough with skill, but by someone who had to be part fool and part optimist. Some of the facets showed a falling away of interest towards the end. There was a Dutch Jew in Tel Aviv who measured up to that kind of temperament. It might be his work.

That hardly mattered. The small, grey-haired man decided on a small experiment with the Blue Wesselton and chuckled to himself. It would be amusing to play around a little with the stone before it was discarded. Things had gone well lately; no one would complain.

Removing the Light Cape from under the microscope, he got up, glanced with casual disinterest at the panorama of mountains and lake outside the broad window of the studio room which was his workshop, then padded on slippered feet to the equipment waiting on another bench.

Another two weeks, they had told him, and his task would be over. The tension would end.

Until the next time.

There always seemed to be a next time, and he was always too greedy, too frightened to refuse.

CHAPTER ONE

It was a warm, sunny September day on the south coast of England, the view from the window table at the restaurant bar was of a yacht harbour filled with a forest of masts and rigging, and as far as Andrew Laird was concerned the only thing spoiling it all was the heavily built, middle-aged man sitting opposite him.

It was the first time he had met Bullen Thoms. He had spent half the morning driving down from London for their meeting at Poole, on the Dorset coast. Bullen Thoms, a respected London shipbroker with an expensive lifestyle, had wanted it that way. It had taken only a few moments for Laird to discover an active dislike for Thoms, a patronising, aggressively self-important individual.

But the irony of it all was that Laird had driven that south coast route feeling almost sorry for the man, not looking forward to what he was going to have to do to him. His mission was simple enough— to destroy Bullen Thoms.

"The way things are in the shipping world, any business is good business." Thoms had been talking and had paid for the drinks. Nursing his almost empty glass, he gave Laird a leer of a grin. "But you could say I'm getting my share—of most things."

"I've heard that," said Laird.

As a marine claims adjuster with Clanmore Alliance Assurance, he'd read a lot more. Most of it was in the thick file in the battered briefcase at his feet. As a dossier, it branded the shipbroker as a thief, a liar, and worse.

"Then maybe you've also heard I don't like my time being wasted." Thoms finished what was left of the whisky in his glass at a gulp, then set it down. "You wanted this meeting. How about telling me why?"

"Here?" Laird looked around the busy restaurant bar. Sunlight was pouring in through its big tinted-glass windows. It was noon and the kind of warm, cloudless day the south of England often produced in early September. "You might want to hear this in private. That's why I suggested your office."

"Back in London?" The man's fat, probably once handsome features twisted in derision. "Understand this, Laird. I put a lot of shipping insurance in Clanmore Alliance's direction. So if you want to see me when I'm having some time off, then I decide where." He gestured at the other crowded, noisy tables. "This place is fine. Real privacy is in the middle of a mob."

"Your choice." Laird sipped his beer for a moment, considering the man.

They were opposites in just about every way imaginable. Laird, just approaching his thirtieth birthday, over medium height and stockily built, had thick dark hair which was prematurely grey at the temples. His grey-green eyes had faint crow's-foot lines of living beneath them, his nose had been broken and reset, he had long, strong-fingered hands, and his voice still held a native Scottish wisp. Bullen Thoms, a man beginning to thicken around the middle, was medium height with close-cut fair hair. His eyes were small and restless, his hands were pudgy. Laird wore a business suit as if it didn't really belong to him, whereas Bullen Thoms looked totally at home in an open-necked white shirt, white trousers, and a blue blazer with black buttons. In the sailing world black buttons were reserved for yacht owners.

Thoms certainly owned a yacht. His forty-foot motor cruiser, the *Iden*, was berthed at a pontoon only a minute away from the restaurant bar. The Clanmore file told a lot more about him. Shipbrokers were the middlemen who found cargo for ships and ships for cargo, usually making a substantial profit both ways of the deal. Bullen Thoms was no exception. Married and moneyed, he had a prestige office address in London and a mews house in a fashionable part of Chelsea. He bought a new Jaguar coupe every year and dabbled in right-wing politics.

The rest had taken Clanmore's marine claims department almost a year to prove and double-check. Bullen Thoms had been tried, found guilty, and sentenced. There could be no appeal.

He was finished.

A gust of laughter from one of the other tables told that someone's story had reached its comic punchline. Thoms smiled indulgently, conveying that he'd heard it before. Then he waved a casual greeting to some new arrivals heading for the bar counter. They waved back. A woman, in her thirties, dark-haired, wearing a halter top and minuscule shorts, blew him a kiss.

"Someone's ex-wife," explained Thoms casually. "How about another drink—then we start?"

"Not for me." Laird shook his head.

"Suit yourself." Thoms snapped his fingers at a passing waitress and indicated his empty glass. Then, with a grunt, the beefy-faced man got to his feet. "I want a word with someone. Enjoy the view— I'll be back."

Threading his way between the tables, Thoms headed for the bar and the woman in the halter top. He patted her familiarly on the rump, she turned and smiled, and Thoms began talking to her.

Laird sighed and switched his attention to the boats outside. They were there by the score. A new arrival, a small, gaff-rigged cutter, was rippling in towards the quayside crewed by three bronzed girls in bikinis. That involved sliding past another boat where a lanky, bearded man wearing shorts and a yachting cap was loading cases of beer aboard.

The bearded man might be setting off for a few days' cruise across the Channel and along the French coast, or starting a single-handed trip around the world. Either way, Poole Harbour would regard it as routine. Rated as one of the finest and largest natural yacht basins in Western Europe, an almost land-locked bay measuring four miles by seven, always with a few thousand yachts either at resident berths or visiting moorings, Poole had a few other claims to fame but didn't need them.

Returning with Bullen Thoms's ordered drink, the waitress leaned across the table in a way that left Laird looking down the front of her dress while she set down the glass.

"Left on your own?" she asked sympathetically.

"The way you see it." He smiled at her.

"Business visit?"

Laird nodded.

"I thought so. You don't look like one of his usual friends," she said dryly. "Can I get you anything?"

Laird shook his head and she left.

Bullen Thoms was still over at the bar, talking to the woman, one hand now resting lightly on her shoulder. Laird watched, sipped his beer again, and didn't notice the waitress return or the way she slowed. She intended to talk, then decided against it and kept on going.

But she looked back. The stranger was a change from those usual yacht freaks. When he'd smiled at her, he'd looked almost boyish for a moment—whatever his age. She liked men who could still look that way. She caught herself wondering about that nose.

If she'd asked, Laird would have told her. It had happened one wild night ashore in Hong Kong, when he'd earned his living a different way, sailing deep-sea as a radio operator aboard a salvage tug.

But that was several yesterdays away, marine insurance was something very different, and Bullen Thoms was ambling back from the bar. He sat down opposite Laird again.

"That's one little social problem sorted out." Thoms winked heavily, then leaned his elbows on the table. "So—your turn, Laird. What's worrying you? I haven't any claims hassle going with Clanmore."

"That's not how we see it," said Laird quietly. He met the other man's eyes. "Remember the *Sycure*, Mr. Thoms?"

The man's face twitched in surprise, but he recovered quickly.

"The *Sycure?*" His voice wasn't totally steady. "I haven't handled any ship with that name."

"You didn't handle it up front," agreed Laird. But it was all in the briefcase, from dates and places to names and pay-offs. "Our people reckon you came out of the deal with a clear personal profit of two hundred and twenty thousand—pounds sterling, not dollars."

"What the hell do you think you're saying?" Thoms mustered rage, his words strangled and low. "If that little creep Osgood Morris is behind this—"

"He ran the investigation." Laird hid a wisp of amusement. Osgood Morris, the Clanmore marine claims manager, was certainly a little creep and sometimes worse. But from the moment Morris had scented the first lead in the *Sycure* affair, he had refused to let go. "Do I stick to basics, or do you want fine detail?"

"Go on." Thoms reached for his glass and took a quick swallow, his hand shaking a little. A few drops of whisky dribbled from his lips and ran down the front of his blazer. "But, by God, whatever this is about, it is going to cost someone."

"That's how we see it, Mr. Thoms." Laird watched the man's apparent rage give way to a first hint of apprehension. "The *Sycure* is Panamanian registered, a general cargo ship on the South America–Europe trade. About this time last year she docked at Lisbon with a cargo of Colombian coffee beans. That's when the trouble began. Don't you even remember the stories that went around?"

Thoms moistened his lips. "I'm not sure."

"Well, the problem came when she unloaded," said Laird. "The *Sycure*'s captain discovered he had two different coffee importers waiting on the dockside, each insisting they owned his cargo, each waving every kind of document to prove ownership—and that they'd both paid for that coffee in full the moment it was loaded at the Colombian end." He shrugged, almost mildly. "There's a lot of money in coffee. Someone who knew the system set up an almost watertight fraud and made a fat killing."

"That's happened before," muttered Thoms.

Laird nodded. But most cases of maritime fraud were crude at the edges. What made the *Sycure*'s case unusual was the smooth way in which one set of genuine documentation for her cargo had become two at the same time as two other sets had become one.

Trust and documents—the shipping world operated that way because it had no option. Buyers lodged letters of credit with an overseas bank. Sellers or their agents could draw that letter of credit money the moment they could show the bank a signed bill of lading which said the cargo had been loaded into a ship's hold. The system was called "free on board," and the cargo belonged to the buyer from that moment.

"I don't know a damned thing about any of it," blustered Thoms. He took a quick glance around the other tables to make sure they hadn't acquired an audience in the noisy bar. "Ask anyone in shipbroking. I run a firm with a cast-iron reputation. I've a solid record."

"That's right," agreed Laird. "That made it more difficult—we had to be more than sure."

Lawyers, banks, insurance companies—all had been caught up in the aftermath of the *Sycure* affair. Clanmore had carried the insured risk for one importer, International Fidelity had held the rest of the business. Eventually they'd patched up a compromise and had paid out close to four hundred thousand pounds—small beer compared with some claim situations, but the *Sycure* affair wasn't the kind anyone forgot quickly.

"I've had enough." His voice a hiss, Thoms leaned across the table. "Show me one shred of evidence I even knew about a coffee deal—show me or get out."

Silently Laird took one of the small white napkins from a dispenser on the table, then produced a ball-point pen from an inside pocket. He wrote three names on the napkin. The first was a clerk in the overseas department of a Lisbon bank, the second was a minor government official in Bogotá, the third ran a back-street printshop in London.

He slid the napkin in front of Bullen Thoms. The man glanced at it, and his mouth sagged open.

"Little people," said Laird. "There were plenty more—sign this or do that, take the money and don't ask why. You set it up, you sat back, and we can prove what we say every inch of the way."

A first small bead of perspiration formed on Thoms's forehead and went trickling down a flabby cheek. He crumpled the napkin, stuffed it into his blazer pocket, tried to speak, failed, then tried again.

"Outside." It was a plea.

"Go ahead," said Laird.

Shoving back his chair, Thoms rose and blundered through the bar towards the door. Laird followed him; they went out into the open, and Thoms stopped on the quayside. The gaff-rigged cutter had berthed, her sails were lowered, and the three girls were joking with the man who had been loading beer on his boat.

Bullen Thoms stared at them and saw nothing.

"What will happen?" he asked tonelessly.

"That depends on you," said Laird.

"On me?" Thoms glimpsed hope. "What about the police? Wouldn't they be involved?"

"Not if there was another way," said Laird. "Clanmore believes in the corporate image."

"Too many people left with egg on their faces." Thoms gave a defeated nod of understanding. "So what do you want—what kind of deal?"

"The kind that will balance the books." Deliberately Laird switched his attention to the girls again. They were easy to look at; he didn't enjoy spectating on the way the bulky, badly frightened shipbroker was coming apart. "Clanmore and International Fidelity are both in on this."

Thoms licked his lips. "No prosecution?"

"None. But afterwards you announce you're giving up business—early retirement. You can claim your health isn't good."

It would be a public face-saver, but the word would go out in shipping circles. Bullen Thoms would be finished.

"How much?" asked Thoms.

"The four hundred thousand it cost us—plus expenses."

"My wife doesn't know." Thoms made it a hoarse, almost unintelligible whisper. "And I've a daughter—she's at college."

"Then keep them out of it."

The man swallowed. He walked a few steps along the quayside, stopped at the edge, and stared down at the lapping water. His fleshy lips quivered a little.

"There's a problem." He waited for encouragement, then gave up. "You'll get your money, but I'll need time."

"Don't push your luck," warned Laird. "Osgood Morris isn't renowned for patience."

"It makes no difference, damn him." A brief spark of the man's natural aggression showed, then died. "Look, I hit a bad patch last year—deals that went wrong. Then I got my fingers burned in a charter deal. The firm was in trouble."

"So you pulled the *Sycure* double-header?"

"I cleared enough on it to get me off the immediate hook, but that was all. My boat is mortgaged; so is the house. I'm still clearing a bank overdraft." Thoms bit his lip and eyed Laird. "I need that time—just a few days. There's a way, a couple of people who might help."

"Don't think of running," warned Laird.

"In my state of health?" Thoms made a weak attempt at a smile. "I won't."

"A week, then." Laird kicked at a small stone, and it plopped into the water. A big ocean-going ketch, bright orange sails above a white hull, was catching the sun as she came into the bay. He saw her make a sudden swing to avoid a flotilla of small sailing dinghies and could imagine the cursing. "A week—that's your limit."

"I'll call you." Thoms ran a hand across his twitching mouth. "Thanks. I—"

"Just do it." Laird turned on his heel and walked away.

He'd left the Ford station wagon from the Clanmore staff pool in a sun-baked parking lot reserved for yacht club members. Someone had slapped a curt warning notice on his windshield, and he spared a moment to place it under a wiper blade of the black Rolls-Royce in the next bay. When he opened the Ford's door, it was like an oven inside. Laird took off his jacket and rolled up his shirt sleeves before he got behind the wheel.

Then he sat for a moment, scowling at himself in the driving mirror, thinking of Bullen Thoms. Maybe the shipbroker would come up with the four hundred thousand, maybe he wouldn't. He was being given the chance—and it was more than Laird would have offered him.

But the insurance and banking world often preferred to operate that way, gave priority to covering their losses and keeping down fuss.

Laird sighed and rested his arms on the steering wheel. A stylised tattoo of a Chinese dragon crawled from wrist to biceps on his left arm; a foul anchor with a decorative chain matched it in colour and length on the right. These were two more souvenirs of his time at sea, two more reasons why he saw things differently from people like Osgood Morris.

Standard marine insurance policies still offered shipping coverage against old-fashioned piracy. But the modern world's real sea vultures operated from smart offices on dry land.

They were the real unseen enemy for any seaman. They could finish off their victims as surely as if they'd made them walk a plank; they could be as ruthlessly deadly as any old-time buccaneer—and they cleared a lot more money.

"We'll see." He said it aloud, almost viciously, then started the

Ford, reversed out of the parking space, and threaded his way back to the main road.

His landmark was the tall grey building which was lifeboat headquarters for the whole of the British coast. He reached it, had a last rear-view mirror glimpse of masts in the bay, then began following the signs for the M3 route to London.

He'd eat somewhere on the way. At least it was Friday, and he would have the weekend to himself.

Andrew Laird filed his report on Bullen Thoms at the Clanmore Alliance office late that afternoon. He didn't forget the man over the weekend, but there were other things to occupy his mind.

Saturday and Sunday were spent far away from ships and the sea, at a cottage deep in the heart of Shakespeare country, a few miles from Stratford-on-Avon. The cottage had old oak beams and a thatched roof; it belonged to a red-haired woman doctor who was a consultant anaesthetist, and she was redecorating. Laird worked with scraper and paintbrush; she fed him coffee and sandwiches. They shared the only bed on Saturday night; then there was more painting and scraping before she drove him back to London late on Sunday.

There was no other involvement between them, but they had been friends for a long time.

He spent most of Monday much nearer home, aboard a Norwegian ship which had tied up at a London dockside wharf. The Norwegian had limped in with a gashed bow, her captain protesting it wasn't his fault that he had collided with a French bulk carrier. The Frenchman was still sending out equally angry noises by radio, threatening everything short of war, but eventually some kind of insurance compromise would be hammered out which neither of them would like.

It was late afternoon before he finished and took a taxi back to Clanmore Alliance's city office. A big, shabby stone-fronted building, it occupied most of one side of a Victorian square near to Oxford Street. The nearest neighbours were a foreign bank, a health studio, and a high-class late-night strip club. Some day Clanmore's directors would sell out and move. The right bid might come from an Arab embassy.

Going in, Andrew Laird went through the reception area with its counters and contract-hire greenery. Ignoring the elevators, he walked the three flights of stairs up to the marine department. Clanmore's ten marine claims assessors occupied a large room off the main corridor and shared five desks, a single secretary, a word processor, and two main computer terminal units—a reasonable economy arrangement for a team that spent most of its time away from base, working abroad.

The room was empty, the word processor switched off. Nancy Andrews, the young Jamaican girl who presided over it and ran most other things, decorated her area with pin-ups of muscle men from keep-fit magazines. He saw that someone had sabotaged her collection, giving them curling felt-tip pen moustaches.

That wouldn't have pleased her. He grinned, passed by, and checked the message board. There were several messages for Halliday, on his way back from a ship fire at Hong Kong, a few for most of the others, including Balfour, stuck at some miserable port in the Baltic, but only one slip of paper in Nancy's familiar scribble pinned against his own name.

"See the man."

It didn't need expansion. He grimaced, went along the corridor to the glass door marked Marine Claims Manager, knocked, and went in.

Osgood Morris had a large, managerial status desk with its own built-in V.D.U. terminal. A small, thin man with sparse hair, a sharp nose, and weasel eyes, he looked up, pursed his lips in what was meant to be a welcome, then nodded towards a chair.

"How do things stand with that damned Norwegian?" he asked as Laird closed the door again and settled in the chair. "Does he have much going for him?"

"He thinks so." Laird shook his head. "I don't."

"It can wait." Morris had a high-pitched voice which usually managed to sound petulant. He paused, fingering the solitary sheet of paper which lay in front of him on the otherwise empty desk. He had worked that way ever since the day Clanmore's chairman had circulated a memorandum that a clean desk equalled an organised mind. "I've heard from another of our little problems, Bullen Thoms."

"He's early—he had a week." Laird raised an interested eyebrow. Osgood Morris had wanted a personal report as soon as he'd returned from Poole and had seemed satisfied with the way things had gone. "Is he ready to do a deal?"

"Yes." Morris shifted uncomfortably and chewed his lower lip for a moment. "But not the kind we wanted—you'll have to see him again."

"I thought once was enough," said Laird, puzzled.

"We may have to compromise," Osgood Morris said. "At the very least, we have to listen to him."

"Why?"

"He phoned about an hour ago." Morris looked at the sheet of paper again, crushed it between his fingers, threw it at a waste basket, and missed. "He wants to trade. We forget the money, give him total immunity from prosecution, he tells us everything he knows about another situation—something much bigger."

"Do you believe him?" asked Laird.

"All I believe is that we'd be fools to trust him." Morris sucked his lips and looked even more like a weasel. "But suppose Thoms is genuine? He claims that this—this situation will happen within the next two weeks, with more than one ship involved. The rest of it, all I know, is that he also claims he has only been an errand boy for the people involved—and he made some fairly dramatic noises about what could happen if they found out he'd talked."

"I wouldn't weep for him." Laird accepted the inevitable. "When do I meet him?"

"Tomorrow, ten a.m., Poole again." Morris raised his hand, forestalling protest. "He insisted, I agreed—and we make no contact with his office or his home."

"All right." Laird nodded and thought gloomily of the drive along the south coast route. "What if he wants guarantees from us?"

"None, until we know more about his offer, some solid facts." Osgood Morris paused and glanced almost reverently towards the ceiling. "I've—ah—taken guidance on this."

"There's nothing better, Osgood," said Laird.

The sarcasm was lost. As far as Osgood Morris was concerned, divine guidance was located on the executive floor above. The marine claims manager lusted for a place on Clanmore's board, made no secret of it, and scurried upstairs at any opportunity.

"One final point." Morris paused and looked slightly anxious as Laird got to his feet. "Andrew, I'll rely on you to handle any public situation—ah—diplomatically."

"Don't kick him in front of witnesses?" Laird nodded and left.

Nancy had returned when Laird reached the claims adjusters' room. Another of the team had also arrived. Jerry Reilly, a lanky young Irishman, was clowning around wearing an Arab fez while the Jamaican girl grinned encouragement.

"What happened to your camel?" asked Laird. Reilly had been sent out to Tangier on a claim involving stolen cargo. He hadn't been expected back for another couple of days.

"They don't come house-trained," said Reilly. "Anyway, there wasn't a spare seat on the plane." He removed the fez and tossed it to Nancy, who tried it on. "Our darlin' girl here says you've got the Bullen Thoms thing. How's it going?"

"Early days," said Laird. "How was Tangier?"

"Bad paperwork and a dockside foul-up. You can't steal cargo that was never loaded." Reilly dismissed it with a grimace as he came over. "I did some legwork on the *Sycure* claim, just after Thoms was linked with it. He smelled like trouble."

"He's shaping the same way."

"That figures." The young Irishman gave him a sympathetic wink. "I'm off to see Osgood. I've got to explain to him how Tangier is a terrible expense of a place to visit."

It took Laird half an hour to dictate a tape of his report on the Norwegian ship. By then it was after five, and Reilly still hadn't returned from Osgood Morris's office. Dropping the tape in Nancy's tray, Laird said goodnight, left, and took the elevator down to the basement garage. He signed for the same Ford station wagon, checked that the tank was full, then got aboard, and drove it out into the London traffic.

He spent a quiet night at home, on his own, watching TV, and the only time the phone rang a woman had dialled the wrong number.

Home was a basement flat just off Bayswater Road. It had a living room, a small kitchen, tiny bathroom, and two cupboard-sized bed-

rooms, and he shared the rent with an English engineer who travelled everywhere doing strange things to oil wells. On an average,
their paths crossed about once every couple of months.

There was little worth watching on any of the TV channels, but
he stayed with a creaky old Hollywood epic because the dialogue was
as familiar as faded wallpaper. He could listen from the kitchen
while he fried some cuts of liver and threw in a couple of rashers of
bacon and some flaked onion. Then he went back to the TV screen
and ate with the plate balanced on his knees and a mug of coffee on
the floor at his side.

Tomorrow it was back to Bullen Thoms again. He shrugged, finished the last of the coffee, tidied things away, and poured himself a
modest measure of neat malt whisky from a bottle that belonged to
his absent flat-mate.

Bullen Thoms. Fact or fiction, the man wanted to trade. Why?
Laird's grey-green eyes hardened a little while he watched the comforting flicker on the TV screen. Pay up or go to jail—Clanmore's
approach to the shipbroker came down to a form of refined blackmail, even if it wasn't new. Maybe Thoms couldn't raise the four
hundred thousand in a hurry—how many people could? But maybe
he was simply wriggling, playing his own game, trying to hang on to
what he had.

Trapped but struggling.

The thought touched a nerve. Swallowing the last of the whisky,
Laird got up and switched his way round the TV channels for something to watch.

The shipbroker's personal world had caved in. Twist the situation,
and Andrew Laird knew how it would feel.

Six years had passed since he and the red-haired girl who was now
a red-haired consultant anaesthetist had been young final-year medical students together. Laird, the son of a Scottish sheep farmer, had
been favourite for the class gold medal.

Then it had all gone wrong, for a reason he would never regret.
His mother, in terminal pain, had asked him and had thanked him.
A sympathetic professor had murmured that from one viewpoint the
real crime in mercy killing lay in being caught. Evidence fell short of
police involvement—but there would be no final examinations.

So Andrew Laird had vanished from the medical scene. He had

gone to sea, then had trained as a radio operator. Salvage tugs were vessels where a man with an additional skill in patching wounds wasn't asked questions and was always welcome.

But there had been a girl, a girl who didn't want to marry a sailor. He had left the sea and taken the Clanmore job, and the girl had still finally turned him down. Laird had learned another lesson—never be certain you know what will happen next.

He chuckled to himself, the way he could now, and switched again to the old familiar TV movie.

Bullen Thoms could learn his own lessons.

It was raining hard the next morning, and Laird drove with the blower fan churning to keep the windshield glass clear of mist. Most of the traffic was heading in the other direction, towards London, until near Ringwood. Then most of the British army seemed to be on the move ahead of him. Trucks and personnel carriers, a string of tanks on low loaders, military police snarling around on motor cycles —all combined to slow things down.

When the army decided to play at soldiers there wasn't much anyone could do about it. Laird kept his patience, the convoys at last turned off towards Salisbury Plain, the rest of the world speeded up again, and it even stopped raining.

It was a few minutes after ten when he reached Poole. At the harbour, where the sea looked as grey as the sky, he found a parking space beside a yacht chandlers' store. The wind was whipping in, and he fastened his anorak jacket and turned up the collar as he walked past a first forest of bare masts and bobbing hulls.

The pontoon where Bullen Thoms kept his motor cruiser was next in line. But two police cars and an ambulance blocked the concrete approach, and a small knot of onlookers were being kept off by a barrier rope guarded by a constable. The constable stood with his back to the wind, gloomy boredom on his face. Other uniformed figures were in a group about halfway along the pontoon.

Hands in his pockets, Laird joined the spectators. They were yachting people, and one, a chubby-faced man with several gold chains round his neck and a bag of groceries clutched in his arms, was trying to argue with the constable. He wanted out to his boat. The constable shook his head.

"Irresistible force meets immovable object," murmured a leathery-faced man in blue overalls. "Know him?"

Laird shook his head.

"He's in scrap metal—wall-to-wall money." The man eyed the scene with amusement.

"What's going on?" asked Laird.

"A suicide. They're fishing the body out." The leathery-faced man stuffed his hands in his overall pockets. "It's a man called Thoms—in shipping, owns a motor cruiser. Seems he tied an anchor or something round his neck, then went over the side."

Laird's mouth suddenly felt dry.

"Who found him?"

"A woman. She saw a pair of feet in the water and got curious," said the leathery-faced man casually. He paused and chuckled. The yachtsman with the gold chains and grocery bag had given up and was leaving. "Well, the law won that one."

Laird nodded, but his eyes were on the pontoon. A man and a woman were leaving, the man stockily built, wearing a hairy tweed sports jacket, the woman dark-haired, dressed in a sweater and jeans. Her face was pale; the man was talking quietly to her as they walked.

The last time he'd seen the woman, she'd been laughing and joking with Bullen Thoms at the marine bar-restaurant.

Reaching the quayside, the pair passed within a few feet. The dark-haired woman glanced almost blankly at the knot of onlookers, then seemed to hesitate, giving a slight, puzzled frown, as her eyes met Laird's. But she didn't stop. The man still escorting her, she headed towards another line of boats.

Laird eased back. He found a public telephone kiosk nestling beside a hut a short distance along the marine quayside, fed some coins into the slot, and dialled Clanmore Alliance's London number. In under a minute he was speaking to Osgood Morris.

"I'm at Poole, and we've a problem," he said. "Thoms is dead. Probably suicide."

"Dear God." Morris's thin voice came shocked over the line. "What happened?"

"I'm not sure yet. The police are here." Laird was still fighting down the sick feeling which had gathered in his stomach. "I thought you'd better know."

"Before you meet them?" Morris recovered quickly. "Yes. Obviously we want to cooperate." He paused, and Laird knew the marine claims manager was thinking fast, could almost hear the wheels spinning. "Just use a degree of discretion, Andrew. Clanmore's position—"

"He fell, we didn't push him?" suggested Laird grimly.

"The man was ready to do a deal, we were ready to listen," snapped Morris indignantly. "Suicide? Maybe, but does it make sense? We were giving him a chance—exactly as he'd asked."

Laird took a deep breath and shifted his grip on the phone. He had to admit Morris was right, though that didn't make anything easier.

"Now we've got to deal with what's left." Morris was thinking ahead again, accepting Laird's silence, soothing him along. "I'll handle the London end. Find out all you can on the Poole situation and keep in touch." An edge of fresh anxiety entered his voice. "We'll have to stay with this, learn as much as we can—"

The telephone kiosk had the usual scatter of pencilled graffiti. A couple of the nearest caught Laird's eye while he half-listened to Morris still talking about urgency. *Hang all extremists*, urged some determined reformer. Beneath it, in almost copper-plate script, another student of life declared, *The trouble with business jokes is they get promoted.* He sighed agreement with that.

"Osgood—"

"Yes?" Morris came to an immediate halt.

"I'll call you back." He hung up and pushed open the phone-booth door.

The man with the hairy sports jacket was standing outside. He gave Laird an almost gentle smile, but his eyes were hard and bright.

"Police." The man beckoned with a crooked forefinger. "You were down at the pontoon, weren't you?"

Laird nodded.

"Right." A warrant card came out of the hairy jacket. "Detective Inspector Harkness, Poole C.I.D. Somebody says maybe you can help us."

"Maybe," said Laird. "I don't know her name, but I heard she found him."

"She did. Then she saw you. Any identification?"

Laird handed over his Clanmore Alliance pass. Harkness read it, handed it back, and his manner thawed a little.

"The same lady says she saw you with Bullen Thoms three days ago."

"We talked," agreed Laird. "What else does she say?"

"That she met him afterwards. He was worried sick, said he had to make a trip somewhere, but wouldn't say why. She got the feeling you weren't his favourite person."

Laird nodded. "It was fairly mutual."

"I see." Harkness scraped a thumbnail along his chin and didn't look happy. "You're back again today, and he was a shipbroker. Business?"

"We'd put the frighteners on him," said Laird. "He'd been on the crook, we had him by the proverbials, but he offered to trade his way out."

"So it was like that?" Harkness swore under his breath, then thumbed at the telephone kiosk. "Who were you calling?"

"My boss."

The C.I.D. man considered the concrete at his feet for a moment.

"Marine insurance—does that mean you've sea time behind you?" he asked unexpectedly. "I mean the real kind—not this weekend stuff."

"Some." Laird sensed more behind the question. "Why?"

"I did twelve years, Royal Navy—boy seaman to three-badge man. Then I was fool enough to become a cop. I've a reason, enough of a reason to even show you what we've got. Come on."

Harkness led the way at a fast walk, back to the pontoon, through the rope barrier, and out along the creaking planks until they reached the motor cruiser. A big, well-maintained boat with cream deckwork, the *Iden* was berthed stern-on. A canvas sheet covered something lying on deck near her bow, something that still oozed sea water.

They went aboard. Laird noted polished brasswork, neatly coiled lines, and details like the elaborate Turk's Head splicing on her gangway ropes. Whatever else he had done, it looked as if no one could have faulted Bullen Thoms for the way he looked after his boat.

The door of the midships cockpit swung open, a police sergeant emerged, frowned at Laird, then saw Harkness and relaxed.

"Any luck yet?" asked Harkness.

"Nothing, sir." The sergeant was young, well-fed, had a schoolboy face. He gestured back into the cockpit, at a companionway stair which led down to the for'ard cabin. "I've finished with that end." He glanced at Laird for sympathy. "Not that I know what I'm expected to find."

"Even a little thing like a suicide note would help," said Harkness. "All right, try aft." He saw his sergeant hesitate. "For God's sake, Frank—the back end."

"I'd worked that out," said the sergeant. "Aye, aye, admiral."

He disappeared ahead of Harkness's warning growl. Once he'd gone, Harkness gave a slight grin, then beckoned Laird on, along the deck to the patch of damp and the canvas-covered shape. An edge of leather shoe showed to one side.

"I want you to look at something. But I don't want to tell you what it is, and I'm not playing guessing games," said the C.I.D. man quietly. He made a methodical business of folding back part of the canvas. "There's twelve feet of water under here at low tide—I had to bring in a diver to get him up."

Laird saw why.

In death Bullen Thoms was slack-jawed, wide-eyed, and had what might have been a bewildered expression. The inevitable, unmistakable froth of drowning still coated his thick, sagging lips; water clung to his close-cut fair hair, and a sodden white shirt and cotton trousers clung to his body. A strand of dark green weed had wrapped itself around one of his legs; the gold watch on his wrist, a waterproof yachting model, hadn't stopped.

But it was the rest that mattered. A large, heavy-duty twelve-volt electrical battery lay beside the dead man's head, a smaller strand of the same dark weed caught up in the crudely knotted cradle of nylon rope which tied it round the shipbroker's neck. The battery had the word "Iden" painted on its casing.

Something like an anchor—the stranger on the quayside had been right. Laird shivered and blamed the gusting wind.

"His spare battery," volunteered Harkness. "It's a twin of the one in use. Try lifting it."

Kneeling, using the rope cradle, Laird eased the battery clear of the deck, then gently set it down again. There was enough weight to moor a small boat.

"When did it happen?"

"We've a witness who saw him heading for the boat just before midnight." Harkness moved nearer and squatted down; the movement was enough to cause the motor cruiser to sway a little. "Sometime after that—we'll have to wait for the medical people."

"No one heard anything?"

Harkness shook his head. "Only one other boat on this pontoon had people aboard overnight. They were asleep."

Sitting back on his heels, Laird frowned. A deep abrasion ran like a collar round the soft flesh of Bullen Thoms's neck, the cause simple and obvious. The rope hadn't been tied tightly and had allowed movement. He had a brief, macabre picture of the dead man held head down under the water, of a body tugged and pulled at by tide and current.

But there was still something wrong. He looked at the dead man again, a vague tendril of doubt nagging at his mind for a reason he couldn't quite place. It was something practical, something in front of him, a flaw that shouldn't be there.

"Got a problem?" asked Harkness.

He glanced at Harkness's face, with its total lack of expression. He realised Harkness already knew and was waiting—and suddenly Laird saw the answer.

"Did he have any help on this boat?"

"A paid hand?" Harkness shook his head. "No. Thoms looked after everything on his own." He paused. "Made a good job of it—almost professional."

"Yes." Laird looked along the length of the *Iden*'s beautifully maintained deck. Then, his lips a tight line, he looked down at the crude tangle of knotted rope around the heavy battery, at the bulky, amateurish way it had been tied to Bullen Thoms's neck. "He'd have done a neater job than this."

"That's what I wanted someone else to say," said Harkness. He rose, pulled the canvas cover back in place, then offered his hand as Laird got to his feet. "People call me Sam—once they get to know me."

They shook hands. Harkness took a moment to smooth one edge of the humped canvas between them, then grimaced as another gust of wind came in and brought a clatter from the bare rigging of the yacht at a neighbouring berth.

"We've a few things to talk about," he said shortly. "Let's go below."

They went into the *Iden*'s cockpit and from there down to her for'ard cabin. It was laid out as a day saloon, furnished in a practical style which included a small bar built against one bulkhead, the bottles held secure by tall mahogany fiddle boards. A photograph showed Bullen Thoms in yachting gear. He was grinning at the camera and holding a silver trophy.

"Nothing apparently disturbed aboard. A place for everything, everything in its place." Harkness crossed to the bar, paused, and rubbed his chin with the back of one hand. "Even the booze."

He took two clean glasses from a rack and used his handkerchief to bring out an opened bottle of whisky. Unscrewing the cap, he splashed a generous measure into both glasses, gave one to Laird, then sat back on a leather-covered couch.

"Medicinal." He raised his glass in a wry token toast to the photograph, took a swallow of whisky, then frowned as a muffled clatter came from somewhere aft. "Hell, I forgot about him." He raised his voice. "Frank, come through."

The sergeant soon appeared at the cabin entrance.

"Anything yet?" asked Harkness.

"Damn all, sir." The sergeant wiped at a streak of oily grime on his schoolboy face and made things worse. His hands were filthy. "I went through the sleeping cabin again—"

"It hadn't been used," explained Harkness for Laird's benefit. He turned back to his sergeant. "How much is left?"

"I'm just double-checking the engine compartment." The sergeant wistfully eyed their glasses. "Two thumping big diesels, a work bench, and a locker full of spares."

"Well, get on with it," said Harkness. He turned to Laird again as the sergeant departed. "That business on deck—I had to do it that way."

"I won't quarrel with that." Laird sat on the other couch on the opposite side of the cabin and tasted his drink. Bullen Thoms had kept a good brand of liquor. "There's a word you haven't used yet."

"Murder?" Harkness nodded. "It could be that way." He gave Laird a calculating scrutiny. "How about a trade—your story against mine, as far as they go and off the record?"

"That was going to be my line, Sam," Laird told him.

They exchanged wry grins.

Laird was first. He kept the story to a few brief sentences, shorn of frills, while Harkness listened in total silence. Occasionally the C.I.D. man shaped a surprised frown, and at the finish he sucked his lips for a moment.

"So if Thoms had paid up this four hundred thousand, you'd have closed the books—no police, no prosecution?"

"Clanmore is no different from any other big company—we'd rather wash our own dirty linen." Laird shrugged. "Look, I don't make the decisions. But even if he hadn't paid, even if we hadn't accepted this mystery deal, there's still a chance we'd have done nothing."

"Just made damned sure he was finished? I've heard how it happens. All right, how about this shipping fraud? How often does that kind of thing happen?"

"It's an industry," said Laird wearily. It was, the kind that cost the marine insurance world, ship owners, and innocent outsiders millions every year. "World-wide, several times a week, every week. Sometimes they're large, sometimes they're small."

"And you say Thoms was small-time?"

"Relatively. But he was a shipbroker—we were supposed to be able to trust him. That made the difference."

He watched Harkness digest the fact and left it there. But Clanmore was currently one of four insurance groups on the fringe of a ten-million-dollar fraud involving steel shipments and was simultaneously fighting off liability in another claim in which almost the same value in machine tools had vanished. Government agencies and police were involved in both; no one was getting anywhere.

When a claim came lower down the ladder, it was sometimes better just to pay up and try to smile. That cost less.

"And I worry about house insurance." Harkness sighed. "All

right, go back to this deal he was offering. Isn't there any hint of what he had in mind?"

"Just that it's something big, and soon."

"Which doesn't help." Harkness swallowed the rest of his drink, then balanced the empty glass on the couch beside him. "The autopsy might turn up something. But if it doesn't, what have I got?" He gestured despairingly. "I've a boss who practically needs help to tie his shoelaces. Start talking to him about knots and murder in the same breath, and he'll think I'm crazy." He winced as another loud clatter and a curse came from somewhere aft. "He might even be right."

"I wouldn't vote for that." Laird took a long, slow look around the cabin. "When did Thoms get here?"

"Late yesterday, as far as we know." Harkness was curious. "Why?"

"Any sign of a briefcase or an overnight bag?"

"No." The policeman's broad face reddened a little. "I should have thought of that. We've still to check his car." He sucked his teeth for a moment. "Any other happy thoughts?"

"We gave him a week. He had more than half that time left." There was a small black fly crawling along the bulkhead above Harkness's head. Laird watched it at the same time as he heard the gentle rhythmic chuckle of water against the boat's glass-fibre hull. "Suppose he went to someone he thought would have to help him, his last chance, but was turned down?"

"Then took fright at what he'd done and came back here to hide?" Harkness nodded soberly. "It's wild—but wild enough to happen." He stopped there as his sergeant padded back into the cabin. Giving a quick sniff, Harkness wrinkled his nose in disgust. "Frank, do you know you stink?"

"I'm closer to it than you are," said his sergeant gloomily. He scowled down at his damp trouser legs, while the aroma of sour bilgewater filled the cabin space. "You said look everywhere."

"Well, take that pong out of here. Call the station and ask how much longer we've to wait for a police surgeon," ordered Harkness. "Say if one doesn't get here soon, I'll settle for a vet—they're more reliable."

His sergeant gave a resigned nod and left. They heard him stumbling his way up through the cockpit, then along the deck overhead.

"Which leaves you." Harkness turned on Laird, with a grimace of apology. "It's time I threw you back ashore. But you'll stay in touch?"

Laird nodded, finished his drink, and rose.

"I'll do the same," promised Harkness. "When are you heading back to London?"

"Soon." But there was one thing he had to do first. "Mind if I talk to the woman who found him?"

"She may not want to talk to you—that's up to her." Harkness wasn't enthusiastic. "Her name is Ann Rodder; her boat is the *Lady Ann*, two pontoons north of this one." He shrugged. "I didn't get much sense out of her, but I'm going to try again later."

"I'll go easy," promised Laird.

He turned to leave.

"Wait." Harkness stopped him with an awkward gesture. "Straight question, give me a straight answer. Ever miss being away from the sea?"

"Now and again," admitted Laird. "You?"

"Often," said Harkness. "Specially like now—when a mess lands on my plate."

CHAPTER TWO

The wind was still chopping the surface of the bay, bringing a hint of salt spray, keeping flags and masthead pennants snapping. The last spectators had gone from their side of the barrier rope at the quayside. Only the constable remained, still on guard, and he gave Laird an amiable nod.

A tightly packed line of boats filled the second pontoon to the north with the *Lady Ann* at the seaward end. Her neighbours were a large red powerboat and a small cockleshell of a sailing dinghy.

Laird paused. An old, broad-beamed one-ton class with a varnished, clinker-built hull, the *Lady Ann* didn't seem to have left her berth for some time. But though the rigging blocks clattering against her bare mast showed signs of neglect, her owner was still house-proud. The upperworks and rails had been recently painted, and the deck planking was well scrubbed. He noted the power cable and a telephone line running aboard from the pontoon, and a connected fresh-water hose.

A flicker of curtain at a cabin porthole showed that he'd been spotted. He stepped aboard, the water lapping against the *Lady Ann*'s hull, clear enough to show empty bottles lying on the bottom ooze, then knocked lightly on the cabin door in the stern cockpit.

Nothing happened. He tried again, waited, heard slow footsteps on the other side; then there was a click and the door opened. The dark-haired woman looked out at him, her manner cold and angry.

"What do you want?" she demanded.

"Your help, Mrs. Rodder." He saw her eyes harden and added, "The police know I'm here."

Ann Rodder hesitated. Close up, she was older than he'd realised, the dark hair probably tinted, a minimum of make-up and some mascara around the eyes used to maximum effect. Laird guessed she was in her mid-forties. More important, though her face was pale, she seemed to have recovered from any initial shock.

"My help?" Her lips tightened. "If that's what you wanted from Bullen, it didn't do him much good."

"But he intended to meet me again, Mrs. Rodder," said Laird quietly. "That's why I came today. He didn't have any reason to like me, but that's not why he's dead."

She looked at him in silence for another long moment, then sighed, nodded, and beckoned him in. He followed the woman down into the yacht's low-roofed main cabin. It was furnished like someone's lounge ashore, sheepskin rugs on the polished decking, flowers in a vase, two armchairs facing a large TV set. An opened partition door for'ard gave a glimpse of a sleeping cabin.

"Sit down." She indicated the nearest chair and forced a smile. "Anyone your height makes a place look untidy."

He settled in the chair. Ann Rodder took a cigarette from a small, carved wooden box, used a match to light it, then looked down at him.

"Who the hell are you anyway?" she asked bluntly.

"Andrew Laird—"

She shook her head impatiently. "Are you in shipping?"

"The insurance side."

"I see." She drew on the cigarette, then sat on the arm of the other chair, still cautious but thawing a little. "All he told me was you were trouble—trouble with a few adjectives thrown in. You know that I found him this morning?"

"Inspector Harkness told me." Laird sensed the tight control behind her words. "I'm sorry. It must have been—"

"I'd told him to come round for breakfast." She didn't let Laird finish. "He was late; I thought maybe he'd overslept."

Laird nodded. Her voice held a hint of money spent on good schools; the sweater and jeans had cost money when new. But there was something else about Ann Rodder, something that said she'd already had plenty of experience at being bruised by the world and wasn't ready to have it happen again.

"Do you want to talk about it?"

"Why not?" She made a bitter gesture with the cigarette. "It's simple enough. First I thought he wasn't aboard. Then I saw those feet—just his feet, Mr. Laird, under the water. His feet, then the rest of him, while I stood there, shaking." She gestured again with the cigarette. "No, I didn't scream, Mr. Laird. You know why? Those damned feet looking up at me—they seemed ridiculous, obscenely funny. Can you believe I wanted to giggle?"

"It's called shock, Mrs. Rodder," said Laird softly. "I've seen it happen—it doesn't make you any kind of a monster."

"I didn't feel like one—that made it worse." Suddenly she stubbed the half-smoked cigarette in an ashtray, then straightened. "You want help. All right, what kind?"

"Background—let's begin with you. How long have you lived on this boat?"

"About a year." She grimaced. "The *Lady Ann* was about all I could grab in my divorce settlement. My husband managed to make just about everything else disappear over the horizon."

"What about Bullen Thoms?" Laird asked it carefully. "How would you describe—"

"Our relationship?" The woman considered him calmly. "He was on his own when he came down here. I was—well, available. He wasn't the love of my life, and there were times when he could be a swine. That's all it was, Mr. Laird. What kind of label would you give me?"

"Human." Laird meant it and saw the flicker of thanks in her eyes. "Did he talk about his wife?"

"Sometimes. She didn't know, of course—about us, I mean. But the way he told it, she probably wouldn't have given a damn. She spends most of her time abroad." Ann Rodder shrugged. "But he needed her. Daddy has good business and social connections, gives —gave Bullen the kind of respectability he needed."

"Needed?" Laird raised a quizzical eyebrow.

"He said he'd been through a couple of purple patches in his life before they met up." Ann Rodder's voice took on a bitter edge. "Well, she'll be annoyed, at least. She's in the States—New York, I think. Now she'll have to come home for the funeral."

"He told me he had a daughter."

"At college. The high fees, low pass-marks kind. She's abroad too, improving her Spanish."

Laird moved to safer ground.

"Go back to after I left him on Friday," he suggested.

"He came here, briefly. Then he left. He told me he'd head for London first, but he'd have to go on from there, to see some people."

"Did he say why?"

She shook her head. "And I didn't ask—you didn't, not with Bullen."

Laird nodded. Outside a fresh gust of wind whipped against the *Lady Ann*'s hull.

"When was the next time you saw him?" he asked.

"Last night, at about nine. He came aboard, told me he'd just got back, flopped down in that chair you're in, and I fixed him something to eat." Ann Rodder frowned a little. "The way he was dressed, I think he'd already been aboard his own boat. But he still had his briefcase."

Laird stiffened and stared at her.

"You're sure about the briefcase?"

"Yes." She was puzzled and showed it. "I'd seen it often enough —black leather, brass locks. He took it with him when he left."

"Did he say where he'd been?"

"No. But I knew it was Switzerland again—lately, it was usually Switzerland."

"But if he didn't tell you—" Laird left it there.

"Simple." There was a slight tightness in her voice. "Any time he went abroad, he brought me something—usually the last-minute grab kind of present, nothing big. That wasn't his style." She got to her feet, went through to the for'ard cabin, and Laird heard a drawer open. When she returned, she was carrying a small plastic bag. "He had this in his briefcase for me."

Laird took the bag. Heavily overprinted *Zürich Duty Free Shop*, it contained a still unopened bottle of moderately expensive perfume.

"And this way, you usually knew?"

She nodded.

So Bullen Thoms had looked for help in Switzerland, had gone there, had come back having to think again, having to find a different way out. Already Laird had learned more than he'd hoped for— but there was a chance of still more.

"Ann." He used her first name deliberately. "When he went

away, did he ever leave anything with you to keep, to look after for
him?"

"No. Not if you mean anything important." The idea almost
amused her. "I don't think he trusted anyone that much. I've got
spare keys for his car and the boat, because he was always losing his
own set, but that's all."

"Can I see them?"

She sighed, turned, went again to the for'ard cabin, and returned
with a small white envelope. Laird took it from her. The envelope
was sealed, and Bullen Thoms's signature was scrawled across the
gummed-down flap.

"I told you," she said dryly. "He didn't trust anyone."

Laird felt the envelope, then ripped it open. A bunch of keys on a
plain metal ring fell out into his hand. Two were Jaguar car keys;
another was the type that would fit a cabin door; the one beside it
had to be for the dead man's boat engines. But the last key made
Laird frown. Made of bright, hard steel, it had a narrow shank and
was finely notched for a complex miniature pin-lock.

"What about this one?" he asked.

She came nearer, peered at the key, but shook her head.

"I've no idea what it's for. Sorry."

"Someone will know." Laird kept any emotion from his voice.
The pin-lock key had no maker's stamp, no number, no other identification. But he'd seen that kind of key before. If he was right, it
meant that Bullen Thoms had trusted Ann Rodder much more than
she'd realised. Casually he returned the keys to the envelope and
gave it back to her. "These spares—how often did he need them?"

"At least once every few weeks, sometimes more than that." She
brushed back a strand of loose hair. "I suppose everyone has a blind
spot, and he was so damned methodical in other ways—but he
certainly needed them. He'd come charging round in a panic and
scream that he had to get to London in a hurry and couldn't find his
car keys."

"It can happen," mused Laird. "I've done it." But somehow that
kind of carelessness didn't match with the man he'd met or the file
he'd read. "Why the London trips?"

She shrugged. "Business. I've seen him hardly get here for a weekend when he'd be called back."

"And those spares saved the day." Laird gave a mild, encouraging chuckle. "How long before you got them back?"

"Usually when he returned that evening."

"In another sealed envelope, with his signature across the flap?"

"Yes." Her patience had begun to fray. Tossing the envelope on a ledge, she turned to a porthole and stared at the grey world outside. "Mr. Laird, I think this is a waste of time for both of us."

"Do you?" Laird rose from the chair, went over, touched her arm, and felt her stiffen. "Ann, he's dead. Maybe you don't owe him much, but don't you want to find out why?"

"I—" She bit her lip, and just for a moment the mask covering her feelings slipped again. "I don't know. If it was suicide—"

"We don't even know that for sure yet, do we?" Laird didn't wait for an answer. "Right now, anything helps—whether it matters is something for later."

"All right." She turned and faced him and gave a slight shrug. "Go on."

"You got that present of perfume from his last Swiss trip. What about the other times?"

"Different things. More often than not it would be a bottle of some kind, and we'd drink it."

"Jewellery?"

She almost laughed. "No chance."

"Then anything different, anything you've kept?" persisted Laird.

Ann Rodder gave a slow nod. "I've one thing, I suppose. He gave it to me about three months ago, for my birthday—he got back the night before. But—"

"Can I see it?"

"If it does any good." She led him through to the sleeping cabin. There was a bed instead of bunks, with the duvet cover crumpled in a way that showed she'd been lying on top of it. Two lockers had been converted to a dressing table with a mirror above, the glass top littered with make-up jars and oddments. She glanced at Laird. "I'm not the world's tidiest person."

He watched as she opened one of the lockers, reached in, and drew out a small china figure of a cow. She placed it carefully on the glass top and looked at him.

"That's it."

The china cow had a cheerful face, was painted brown and white, and had a scrap of blue and red ribbon tied around its neck.

"Lift the tail," she invited.

The tail was long, straight, and on a small hinge. Cautiously Laird eased it up with a forefinger. There was a click, a whirring pause, then the tinny notes of "Edelweiss" came from a music box hidden somewhere inside the china cow's body.

"Satisfied?" asked Ann Rodder as the tune ended in another whirr and the tail lowered again. "There's nothing else—he was probably drunk when he bought the thing." Her voice softened. "Still, I like it."

"But he didn't say where it came from?"

"No." She put the china cow back in the locker, closed the door, and straightened. "That's my personal souvenir of Bullen Thoms. Not much, is it?"

"But you still knew him better than most people," said Laird quietly. "Ann, what kind of mood was he in last night?"

"That policeman, Harkness, asked me the same thing." She paused, and for several moments there were only the gentle, creaking noises of the boat. "Bullen—well, he was making confident noises the way he always did. But I think he was nervous underneath."

"Nervous?"

"Nervous—or frightened."

Laird sensed it was time to stop.

"How about you—now?" he asked.

"I'm a survivor, Mr. Laird." She said it flatly, but her eyes were bitter. "I'll work at it."

She didn't move as he left.

There was more rain on the way. A whole new armada of heavy clouds was moving in as Laird crossed from the *Lady Ann* to the pontoon boardwalk and set off towards the shore. He needed a telephone; he had to talk to Osgood Morris in London. But as he neared the concrete start of the quayside, Harkness's sergeant ambled out from the shelter of a hut.

"Mr. Laird." The sergeant looked cold and kept his hands in his pockets. "I've a message for you from my boss. We've checked Thoms's car, but there's no luggage aboard it."

"Tell him Thoms had a briefcase last night," said Laird. "And a certain lady has a bunch of keys he should know about."

"Briefcase, keys." Harkness's sergeant didn't look happy but nodded. "Just that?"

"It should be enough. But you can say I'll be in touch—and that I'd have used a bowline." Laird had to grin at the sergeant's puzzled face. "It's a knot. He'll understand."

They parted, and Laird walked on until he reached the same public telephone he'd used earlier. This time he had to stand outside, back to the wind, while two teenage girls in sweaters and slacks giggled their way through a shared call. At last they finished, came out, and Laird took their place. The narrow, glass-walled box still reeked of scent as he dialled the Clanmore number in London.

"How do things look?" asked Osgood Morris when he came on the line.

"Not good," said Laird. "Maybe murder."

"Damn the man." The marine claims manager groaned at the news. "Couldn't he have just died like anyone else?" Then he recovered. "Still, it makes a different situation. It might get us off any kind of moral hook in terms of responsibility, eh?"

"Moral hooks are your department, Osgood." Laird scowled at the telephone mouthpiece. It had lipstick on the edges. "Are we still interested in the deal Thoms talked about?"

"That 'something bigger'?" Morris's voice made it a near squeak. "Yes, of course—maybe more than ever. We have to be. What have you got on it?"

"A couple of start points. He spent the weekend somewhere in Switzerland, and he left some keys with a woman. One looks like a safe-deposit key—no markings—but the box could be in London."

"Do the police know?"

"They will."

"London." Morris sounded thoughtful over the line. "I'll presume Thoms used his own name—no reason why he shouldn't. Perhaps—yes, perhaps we can help a little." His manner became brisker. "Are you heading back now?"

"As soon as I hang up," Laird told him.

"Then I'll get on with it," said Morris.

Laird heard the click as Morris's receiver went down. The line went dead, then changed to a dialling tone, and shaking his head he replaced his own receiver.

He knew what Morris meant and exactly what he was going to do.

Three highly competitive worlds—insurance, banking, and private security—met on many areas of common ground. There were regular situations when they operated their own private mutual aid network—a network each would have solemnly sworn didn't exist.

But it did, functioning like a highly select club with membership at senior management level, blending past favours remembered with the uneasy knowledge that any one of them could be next in line with a problem.

Osgood Morris had membership and was going to use it.

It was raining again as the Ford station wagon left Poole, heading towards the M3 for London.

Laird drove with the windshield wipers slapping and the car radio tuned to a music station, the volume down low. He knew he should have been thinking about Bullen Thoms, but somehow it was Sam Harkness who kept intruding into his thoughts. The bulky detective inspector's nostalgia for the kind of life he'd known at sea wasn't unique. There were many like Harkness, settled in a new life ashore, glad it was that way most of the time, yet never really able to forget.

Particularly when things went wrong. Laird hummed a little under his breath, feeling amused. Sometimes, faced with yet another day at Clanmore, he was tempted to run. More than once he'd been ready to take a berth on any rust-bucket cargo tramp, sailing anywhere—and it might yet happen that way.

Traffic was light between the weather and time of day. Laird eased the Ford out to overtake a heavy truck rumbling ahead and automatically glanced at the rear view mirror. A dark blue Volkswagen van he'd noticed before was still the only other vehicle behind him in the poor visibility; then the rain blotted out the rest of the road in a haze.

The truck, loaded down with crates, had a bright yellow cab and body and was throwing up a thick wake of spray. He could see the way the road began an elbow-like bend some distance ahead, but the margins were safe. Feeding the station wagon more acceleration, Laird passed the yellow truck and left it behind.

Suddenly, unexpectedly, another vehicle was up beside him, over-taking him in the downpour, while that bend ahead loomed up. It was the blue Volkswagen van, the driver a vague shape hunched behind the wheel, still not cutting in. Cursing, Laird started to brake; then the side-loading door of the van slid open a few inches. He saw the twin barrels of a sawn-off shotgun poke out and sensed as much as saw the crouching figure behind them.

A hammer-blow seemed to hit the Ford's windscreen, and the glass cracked and caved into a broken mosaic of quivering particles. His forward view was blotted out; the Ford was skidding; the world switched to a lurching nightmare in which only two things mattered —the corner ahead and the truck thundering along somewhere be-hind him.

Instinct was faster than thought. Punching a fist at the cracked glass, Laird smashed a hole through it. Particles deluged everywhere; the skid had become an aquaplaning spin on the wet road surface, but he could see again.

Wrenching at the steering wheel, pumping the brakes, he fought to regain control, felt the station wagon buck as it hit something hard at the verge of the road, and caught a glimpse of a waiting downward slope and water. The Ford bounced, shook, began to spin again; then somehow he had pulled it round and felt the tyres regain their grip.

Stalling, the Ford shuddered to a stop, which left it broadside across the road. The radio was still murmuring music; the rain was soaking in. He realised that the yellow truck had pulled in behind him—and the blue Volkswagen had gone.

A fist knocked urgently on the unbroken glass of the driver's door. The white face of the truck driver stared in; then the door was hauled open as Laird switched off the radio.

"Are you okay, pal?" The truck driver looked as shaken as Laird felt. He took a gulping breath, glanced at the shattered windshield and the sharp pebbles of glass littering the front seats, then stood back, the rain already soaking his jacket and running down his fea-tures. "Hell, I hit those brakes, but I still thought I'd flatten you."

"I'm glad you didn't. I'd enough problems," said Laird in a wry, hoarse voice he hardly recognised as his own.

He got out of the car into the downpour, more glass falling from his clothing. Other traffic had stopped behind them but was beginning to crawl past. One of the Ford's front tyres had burst; he could see the long gash the car had torn in the roadside grass and just how near he'd come to the edge of that drop.

"That damn Volkswagen," said the truck driver, still beside him. "The wheels must have thrown up a stone chip—I've had it happen. Hits you like a bullet, eh?"

So the man had seen nothing else. Laird's mouth tightened.

"Did you get his licence number?" he asked.

"In this weather?" The man shook his head. "Anyway, pal, what good would it do to cause a hassle? Be glad you're in one piece." He used a wet sleeve to mop his face. "Better get your car in off the road. I'll help you with that tyre."

It took about five minutes to fit the spare. By the time they'd finished, the rain storm had passed, the sun had made a surprise appearance, and the dampness was beginning to steam from their clothes. Waving aside Laird's thanks, the truck driver climbed back up into his cab, gave a farewell blast on the horn, and drove away.

Returning to the Ford, with that raw-edged, gaping hole where the windscreen had been, Laird cleared away more of the glass from the front seats, then got in, closing the door, and sat for a moment.

He hadn't imagined it. The shotgun had been there, that blur of a man behind it in the rain. Yet a shotgun blast at that range—

He should be dead. Unless—

Eventually, searching among the broken glass, Laird nursed half a dozen tiny lead pellets in the palm of his hand. The gun had been loaded with the smallest gauge of birdshot, one size above basic dustshot.

Birdshot. The gunman hadn't meant to kill him, at least not that way. A car crash would have been easier, neater, whether he was left dead or just a hospital case.

Laird shivered, turned over his hand, and sucked the blood on his knuckles where they'd been cut when he'd punched through the windscreen.

Why? The only reason had to be Bullen Thoms.

A windy, uncomfortable drive from there took him to a service station close to the start of the M3 motorway. It had a workshop which stocked temporary plastic sheeting windshields. While one was being fitted, Laird cleaned up in the service station washroom, had a cup of lukewarm coffee from a machine, then used a pay phone to call the police station back at Poole.

Harkness was still out. Laird left a brief message, one that wouldn't gladden the ex-sailor's heart, then hung up as the policeman at the other end began asking questions. Harkness would be told—but even Harkness couldn't perform miracles, and blue Volkswagen vans were an everyday part of the scenery in the south of England.

A few minutes later he was on his way again. The thin plastic sheeting in front of him shivered and rippled and let in draughts at the edges, but it held all the way up to London. At mid-afternoon, he reached the Clanmore Alliance office, drove down into the basement garage, and parked. Nodding to the garage attendant, he crossed to the elevator and rode it up to the third floor.

Jerry Reilly was sitting on the edge of a desk when Laird walked into the marine claims assessors' room. The young Irishman gave him a quick scrutiny, then gave a wry, relieved grin.

"I heard you were on your way up." Reilly gestured towards the phone beside him. "Welcome back—the word was you'd had trouble. A cop named Harkness came in shouting about someone using you for target practice. You're to call him—he sounded like he was sorry they missed."

"They weren't trying too hard—not the way you mean," Laird told him bitterly.

"He said that was your message." Reilly nodded. "Look, I know about Bullen Thoms—Osgood told me. But if that was supposed to be a suicide, if there's still no real proof either way—"

"Why blow it?" Laird asked. "He'd had that same puzzle on his mind all the way up the motorway. "You tell me, Jerry."

"And why you?" Reilly gave up. "Well, if you're fit, then you're not stopping. Osgood wants you at the Hammerman's Trust branch in Mayfair—he's there now, waiting."

"Got an address?" asked Laird.

"Here." Reilly gave it to him on a slip of paper. "What about your pal Harkness, if he calls again?"

"Tell him you haven't seen me."

"I haven't seen you," agreed Reilly. "Anything else I can do?"

"There's a car in the basement that needs a new windscreen."

"No problem." Reilly grinned as Laird laid the keys on the desk. "I'll take care of it personally—I need an excuse to get out for a spell. Uh—I could use the car this evening. All right if I do that, then drop the thing off at your place, later on? I've a date tonight and—"

"Go ahead," said Laird resignedly.

"Thanks." The young Irishman winked. "Those women keep chasing me. It's a problem, Andy."

"You should be in a cage, at a zoo," said Laird.

He left while Reilly was still trying to think of an answer.

The Loyal and Ancient Hammerman's and Weaver's Trust Company of London had stolen its name from two of the old city trade guilds, had half a dozen branches placed strategically across London, and offered what it claimed was the ultimate in security to any customer who wanted to lock up his or her valuables by the week, month, or year. The Hammerman's Trust didn't ask if the customer was concerned about theft or the taxman. It rented out safe deposit boxes, it protected them with armoured vaults, electronics, and a hand-picked staff of uniformed guards who were all ex-policemen.

It charged accordingly.

The Mayfair branch was located in a quiet lane off Hill Street, close to the dignified frontage of the Naval Club. Its nearest neighbours included foreign trade missions, a gaming club, and two charities with royal patrons.

Laird paid off his taxi outside the club and walked from there past the inevitable parked clutter of Rolls-Royces with C.D. plates, messenger motor cycles, and delivery vans. Once in the lane, he walked the last few yards, aware that he was probably being watched by a TV surveillance camera.

The Hammerman's Trust door had a simple metal nameplate. It swung open by remote control when he pressed a button, then closed firmly behind him the moment he stepped inside. He was in a small, carpeted, brightly lit hallway with another door, metal and blank-faced, at the other end.

"Your name, sir?" said a polite female voice.

"Laird, Clanmore Alliance." There was a camera lens above the metal door, but he couldn't decide where the voice came from.

"You're expected, Mr. Laird."

The metal door purred open. Beyond it, a guard was waiting at the start of a comfortably furnished reception area. Laird walked forward, under a metal-detector arch, and saw a second guard sitting at a console which held half a dozen flickering monitor screens.

The guard saluted, led him across to a desk, and the young, smartly dressed woman on the other side had him sign a visitor's slip. As he looked up again, she smiled and he heard the click of a camera shutter. The lens was in the wall behind her.

"Routine, Mr. Laird," she explained.

"No exceptions?"

"None." Her eyes twinkled. "The negative has time, date, and the same number as your visitor slip. Just a precaution." She glanced at the guard. "Tommy will take you through—the other gentleman arrived a few minutes ago."

Puzzled, Laird turned and followed the guard across the reception area and through another set of remote-controlled doors. A stairway with ceramic-tiled walls led to one more door, with a guard at a desk on the far side. In the background the glinting machined steel of the main vault doors dwarfed anything that had gone before. He could hear the hum of air conditioning, and a coffee pot was burbling at the side of the desk.

"All home comforts?" he asked mildly.

"All we need, sir." The guard touched his arm and guided him to the left, then along a short corridor. They stopped at a plain wooden door; the guard tapped on it, then opened the door and ushered Laird in.

It was a small room, with Osgood Morris one of three men seated round a table. The other two were strangers, and as Morris gave Laird a glance and a nod, one of them got to his feet.

"Mr. Laird." He signalled the guard, who went out, closing the door. "Thank you for coming."

"Eventually," said Morris.

"We know why." The stranger gave Laird a not totally happy smile. He was tall, middle-aged, and wore a dark blue business suit with a white shirt and a knitted black tie. "No—ah—ill effects?"

"None." Laird's eyes were on a small steel box lying, closed, on the table.

"I'm glad." The man pursed his lips. "Introductions, I think." "I'm John Laslow, group manager for Hammerman's Trust." He gave Morris a sideways glance. "When I got here and we—ah—investigated a little, we agreed we needed an expert. Someone I—we could trust." He turned to the older man beside him, and the smile returned with an edge of relief. "Miguel Holly is our expert. He's also a friend of mine."

"You're getting long-winded, John," warned Holly. He had a mop of grey hair, thick spectacles, and a lined, cheerful face. Hands deep in the pockets of a crumpled tweed jacket worn over a faded sweater and baggy corduroy trousers, he eyed Laird sympathetically. "People shot at me in a war once, Mr. Laird. It wasn't nice."

Laslow waved Laird into the vacant chair, settled back in his own, then cleared his throat a little.

"Your company made an unusual request, Mr. Laird. But the reasons were sound. I've been assured of total secrecy—"

"Otherwise you wouldn't be here, wouldn't have authorised it," said Morris, his thin voice edging on impatience. "I'm grateful." He turned to Laird. "You were right about that key. Thoms rented a safe deposit box here—"

"Under his own name, perfectly legally," said Laslow quickly. "Under the Trust rules, even police would need a court order before we could open it."

"Once they found it existed," agreed Morris. He reached out and laid a hand lightly on the metal box. "But we've got it, we've opened it. Take a look."

He lifted the hinged lid, and Laird stared, lips shaping a silent whistle of surprise.

In two rows of four, carefully spaced, nestling on a layer of white cotton wool, eight large diamonds sparkled up at him under the cold glow of the overhead tube lighting. They varied in size, in shape, even in colour. But any one of them seemed as if it could be worth a year's pay.

"Like them?" asked Miguel Holly casually.

"Laird lifted one of the stones, held it between his fingertips for a moment, then replaced it in the cotton wool nest.

"Are they—"

"Real?" Holly's eyes twinkled behind the thick spectacle lenses. "Yes. They're diamonds. All between eight and ten carats." He spread both hands in an apologetic gesture. "The trouble is, they're tarted-up rubbish."

Laslow stared at him, Osgood Morris made a spluttering noise, and both totally ignored Laird's bewilderment.

"What do you mean, rubbish?" Morris leaned forward indignantly. "You said—"

"I know." Holly gave him a sad smile. "I said they were good-looking stones. Then Mr. Laird arrived." He shook his head. "I'm sorry, but that's the way it is. These started life as poor-quality, badly flawed diamonds. They've been treated, given a cosmetic job. A good one, good enough to fool a lot of people who think they know about diamonds—and if you don't believe me, maybe you should get a second opinion. I can give you a few names."

"No," said John Laslow firmly. He glanced at Osgood Morris, who was chewing his lip. "You wanted an expert. Miguel is one of the top half-dozen gemmologists in this country—I'm ready to take his word."

"I—" Morris turned to Laird for support, saw none, and almost groaned. "I don't understand."

"Rough diamonds come from the mines in all sizes, all qualities, different colours," said Holly patiently. "They're sorted out by the mining corporations, then at the diamond bourses—the market-places. What we call rubbish is rejected, ground down for industrial use, or sold cheaply." He thumbed at the box. "Stones like these would be rejects. They might be bought to be cut down, to produce a few very small stones each, at a modest price for a modest profit."

No one spoke for a moment. The tube lights overhead hummed faintly; the diamonds sparkled up from their box with a mocking brilliance.

"All right, they're cheap and nasty by your standards," said Laird unemotionally. "Suppose they were genuine. How much would they be worth?"

"That's difficult to say." Holly removed his spectacles, examined them thoughtfully, then replaced them carefully on his nose. "Find the right buyer at the right time—yes, I'll guess and say somewhere over two hundred thousand pounds, maybe up to a quarter of a million."

Laird nodded his thanks. Bullen Thoms had cleared exactly that sum on the *Sycure* fraud. Either he'd settled for the diamonds as a portable investment, made the buy through some underworld deal, and had been cheated in the process, or he'd bought knowing what he was getting and hoping to unload the stones when necessary at a rocketing profit.

But Osgood Morris still needed convincing, still eyed Holly doubtfully.

"You're absolutely sure?" he persisted.

"I earn my living by being sure," said Holly. "If I were buying these stones, knowing what they are, I might be generous and go to ten thousand pounds for the lot—no more. If you want proof, I can give you that under laboratory conditions. In fact"—he glanced hopefully at Laslow—"John, that might be interesting."

"They can't leave this vault." The Hammerman's Trust general manager showed his horror at the thought. "If anything happened, we'd be in a disaster situation. Even going this far—"

"I could do it here, tomorrow," suggested Holly. He drew the box over and looked down at it with unconcealed interest. "I'd enjoy it. Whoever faked this lot is good; I'd like to see exactly what was done."

Laslow hesitated, then nodded.

"Ten a.m. then." Holly was pleased. "Would you like to be a witness, Mr. Morris?"

"I can't. I've a meeting with our chairman." Morris pursed his lips. "But I'd like Laird to be present."

"Good. Miguel Holly closed the box and pushed it back into the centre of the table. "Now can I ask a question? Had this man Thoms any contact with the diamond trade?"

"None we know about," said Laird. "But there could be a Swiss connection."

"Swiss?" The grey-haired gemmologist wrinkled his nose at the thought. "Unlikely—not impossible, but unlikely. London, Amsterdam, maybe even Tel Aviv, I might believe." He produced a jeweller's eyeglass from one pocket and tossed it idly in the palm of one hand. "Even with this, I can tell you that we're talking about an artist. I'd like to meet him."

"So would I," said Osgood Morris. He glanced deliberately at his watch, then got to his feet. "Laird will be with you tomorrow." Turning, he shook hands with Laslow. "Thank you for stretching the rules. I'll—ah—remember it."

"So will I," said the Trust official. He smiled at Laird, who had also risen. "But if we've helped, that's enough for now. Just don't ask me to get any more involved."

They said goodbye to Holly; then Laslow went with them to the door. The same guard was waiting outside to lead them back the way they'd come.

Osgood Morris didn't utter a word until they had left the Hammerman's Trust building and were walking on Hill Street, heading towards Berkeley Square.

"Why did these people shoot at you?" he asked, scowling at an innocent passer-by. "What kind of dividend was there in it?"

"Maybe I'm supposed to know something—or have something."

"Do you—have you?" Morris asked. "If there is anything—"

"No." A large black Cadillac with Arabic numberplates and heavily tinted windows purred past while Laird resisted the temptation to shove Morris under it. "Look, Osgood—"

"I had to ask." Morris didn't make it an apology. "We'll presume they picked you up at that damned marina at Poole." He stopped suddenly and his weasel face lightened. "We don't know what Thoms was saying. He could have claimed he was in a blackmail situation—yes, that you were squeezing him, that he had to buy you off."

"Then somebody in Switzerland says no and decides to get rid of us both?" Laird winced. "Thanks for the thought."

Morris grunted. "He had these diamonds hidden away. He was wriggling, trying to hold on to what he had. The damned fool just wriggled too much." He began walking again. "His family are abroad—you know that?"

Laird nodded.

"But there's still his home in Chelsea, and his office." Morris flagged a passing taxi. It drove straight on and he scowled. "The police have been at both since this morning. They found nothing—and I know the detective who ran the operation. He found nothing."

"And he knew what he was looking for?"

"Yes." Morris flagged another taxi with better luck. "But maybe his secretary is worth talking to on this Swiss thing. We've still our own interests to protect, so try her."

The taxi had stopped, engine ticking.

"Now?" asked Laird indignantly.

Morris nodded, opened the taxi door, and got in.

"One suggestion," he said pompously, still holding the door, leaning forward in his seat. "You've blood on your shirt. Do something about it, Andrew—we've all got standards to maintain."

The door closed, he sat back, and the taxi growled away.

Laird glanced down at his shirt, then watched the taxi disappear round the edge of the Square. He knew Morris and he knew his moods, knew how far he could trust him.

This time he had a prickling feeling that the marine claims manager knew something, was holding it back—and wasn't doing it for Andrew Laird's benefit.

CHAPTER THREE

Bullen Thoms had operated his shipbroking business from a third-floor office within sight of the Inter-City bulk of Euston railway station. Laird got there by Underground from Green Park, handed over his ticket at the Euston barrier, then emerged into sunshine and a noisy protest march being herded along by a few bored police. The demonstrators were hospital workers, about two hundred of them, complaining about job cuts, and he had to wait until their banners and shouts had passed before he could cross the last few yards.

The office building was modern concrete and glass, the tenants on the directory board a mixture of professional and commercial, from two law firms to a video film distribution company. A commissionaire stopped him at a desk in the lobby and frowned when Laird explained what he wanted.

"They've had some bad news, sir." He made it a warning. "I don't know if Mr. Thoms's secretary is seeing anyone."

"The bad news is why I'm here," said Laird with suitable gravity. "Tell her I'm from Clanmore Alliance and that I was at Poole this morning."

The man's face showed a flicker of interest. Turning away, he used the telephone on his desk, spoke briefly, then came back.

"Go straight up, Mr. Laird." He didn't hide his curiosity. "The police were here this morning. They said he drowned, fell off his boat or something."

"Something like that."

"Do you know her—his secretary, I mean?"

Laird shook his head. "Not even her name."

"She's Miss Banks—Jean Banks, a damn nice woman once you get to understand her." The commissionaire thawed a little. "But then she's older, you know what I mean. Why she stayed workin' for that character so long—" He stopped with a grimace. "None of my business. Sorry."

"But you didn't like Thoms much?"

The grimace became a slight grin. "Mister, on this job you get so you don't like anyone."

The elevator was small, like a stainless steel coffin. Laird took it up to the third floor, got out, and found a door marked *Thoms Shipbroking* immediately across the corridor.

He went in. The general office area was a bright, functional layout with about half a dozen desks and the usual filing cabinets. A young, pimple-faced clerk began ambling towards him but stopped as a middle-aged, smartly dressed woman appeared and gave him a glance of dismissal.

"Mr. Laird?" She had a thin, angular face and short, dark hair flecked with grey. "I'm Jean Banks. The commissionaire said—"

"That I had to see you." Laird looked past her. The young clerk and a girl who had been typing at one of the desks were both watching with open interest. "Could we talk somewhere, privately?"

She pursed her lips, then nodded. "Of course."

Laird followed her past the desks and into a large, comfortably furnished private office. He looked around as she closed the door.

"This was his office," she said. "It's—well, you said private."

"Yes." He guessed the woman was in her early fifties. Medium height, she had kept her figure, but her only apparent make-up was a slight touch of lipstick. Her charcoal grey two-piece suit, with a white shirt-blouse, was plain in cut and style—ideal secretary wear. She seemed slightly puzzled but totally composed. Laird glanced around. The main item in the room was Bullen Thoms's desk, but there was also a glass coffee table with low seats. He nodded towards them. "I think we should sit down for this."

"I'm not quite sure what 'this' is, Mr. Laird." She frowned at him. "But you were there when—?"

"I was supposed to meet Bullen Thoms this morning, at Poole." He shook his head. "They'd found his body before I got there."

"I see." She went over, sat down, smoothed the front of her skirt as Laird joined her, and considered him carefully. "The police wouldn't say much about what had happened. Can you tell me?"

"How much does it matter?" asked Laird.

"To me, personally?" She glanced past him, towards the dead shipbroker's desk. Her angular face was hard to read. "I've been with him five years. He paid reasonably well, but I earned it. I—no, I didn't really like him very much. Why?"

"It looked like suicide, but maybe it wasn't," Laird told her deliberately.

"But you don't mean an accident?" She kept tight control and fiddled for a moment with a small gold signet ring on one finger. "What do the police say?"

"They're not certain one way or the other—yet."

"But you are?" Jean Banks looked up at him, frowning. "What do you want, Mr. Laird? I know Clanmore Alliance. We've insured a lot of ships with you, but—"

"Your boss was up to his neck in a cargo fraud, a deal he organised on his own. I met him last Friday and told him we knew. He wanted another meeting today." Laird paused deliberately, watching the woman. "He was offering us a trade, information about something else."

"I wondered." Her eyes strayed towards the empty desk again, its baskets empty, everything waiting neatly in place. Then she sighed and relaxed back in her chair. "You want the honest truth? He was a bastard to work for, an unfeeling bastard. I'd have left a long time ago if anything better had come along. But it didn't."

"And now?"

"This business will just fold up. It's been limping for more than a year; nobody in their right mind would want to move in." Jean Banks shrugged. "The office manager and two of the girls have already got themselves fixed with other jobs. It's about time I started trying too. So—well, ask what you want. I don't think I owe anything here."

She was cool, calm; her whole attitude was totally practical. Probably she had had to be all of these things to stay with Bullen Thoms. Laird found himself thinking of the other woman he'd talked with at Poole. In a different way, they were two of a kind—survivors, stubborn with it.

"How has the business been, financially?" He chose his starting point carefully.

She shook her head. "Not good. Even worse a few months ago, but then he got some outside capital and that kept us afloat."

"Do you know where it came from?"

"No." The woman drew a deep breath. "Look, Mr. Laird, I'll save you some time. I know situations where Bullen Thoms cut a few corners, but that's all—nothing worse."

"But you said, 'I wondered,'" reminded Laird. "Why?"

"Because he'd been spending less and less time here, because I knew he'd been making trips abroad for all sorts of vague reasons—"

"To Switzerland?"

"From the occasional thing he said, yes. He didn't exactly tell me or keep a diary."

"Any names, or places—any hint at all?"

She shook her head, then seemed to hesitate. "Except—no, I can't be sure."

"Tell me anyway," invited Laird.

"A call came through on his private line one day, while he was out. I answered it, and I knew it was a long-distance call—you get that feeling sometimes. The man at the other end said his name was Alton and that Thoms was to call him back." Jean Banks frowned down at her signet ring again, her mouth twisting at the memory. "So I told him when he came in, and he blew up like a bomb—I thought he was going to fire me on the spot. No one, but no one was to answer calls on that private line."

"You'd done it before?"

"Yes. But I didn't after that."

Laird filed the name mentally, then switched from there.

"When did you see him last?"

"Yesterday—Monday. He arrived about mid-day, shut himself in here for about an hour, and I think he used the phone—at least, I heard his voice. Then he left."

"Did he talk to anyone here?"

"No."

"How did he seem?"

"Like it would be sensible to keep out of his way." She said it with dry humour. "I did."

Laird fought down a chuckle. "Did he have a briefcase?"

"Yes—as usual."

"Could he have taken anything from here when he left?"

"The police asked me that. I took a look around and said I didn't know." Jean Banks met his eyes frankly. "I wasn't thinking too straight—they'd just told me he was dead. Maybe I was wrong." She rose from her chair. "I'll show you."

Laird followed her over to Bullen Thoms's desk. It was a heavy dark oak with a grained leather top and had drawers running down each side.

"He always left this one locked." Stooping, Jean Banks pulled open the bottom drawer on the right. It was empty. She glanced round at Laird. "No one else had a key, whatever he kept in it. I—"

She stopped, puzzled, realising that Laird was hardly listening. He reached out and lifted the little porcelain cow which had been lying almost hidden behind the intercom box on the desktop. It had the same lift-up tail and the same scrap of blue and red ribbon tied around the neck. He tried the tail, and the same tinny music began.

"That thing?" Jean Banks winced as the music tinkled on. "He used to play with it till I could almost scream."

"When did it appear?"

"A few months ago, after one of his disappearing acts." She gave a sigh of relief as the music stopped. "He treated it like a mascot, a good luck piece."

Laird put the little figure back on the desk. It was a twin of the one he'd seen on Ann Rodder's boat—no, not the twin, the other half of a pair. This cow had its head turned towards the right; the one on the boat had faced the left.

"Did he say where he'd got it?"

"I asked." Still stooping over the drawer, Jean Banks didn't hide her lack of interest. "He said something about a stall in a giant-sized street market and then some nonsense about nearly being lost in it afterwards."

Laird nodded, though it didn't particularly help. That left the empty, unlocked drawer.

"You've no idea what he kept in there?"

"I just know it stayed locked. It got so I didn't even think about it —at least, not until after the police had gone."

The police had taken Bullen Thoms's desk diary and address book. They'd asked the name of his accountant and had said they'd make sure the shipbroker's wife was told she was now a widow. Laird decided there was nothing else he could do which wasn't already at hand.

But there was a man named Alton somewhere in Switzerland; he had found the second of these ridiculous porcelain cows—and it seemed certain that when Bullen Thoms had left his office, heading for Poole, he'd taken something that mattered, something he might have wanted with him for the deal he was trying to arrange.

Proof of his story, the kind of proof that would let him bargain his way out of trouble?

Except that now he was dead and the briefcase had vanished.

Jean Banks went with him to the elevator when he left.

"Let me know if anything happens," he invited as the elevator door slid open. "Anything at all—call me at the Clanmore office or leave a message."

"I'll call you." She gave a humourless laugh. "Remember, I'm job-hunting. At my age, that's not too easy—I may need an introduction to your personnel manager."

Andrew Laird used a taxi from the Euston station rank for the journey back to Clanmore Alliance. At late afternoon on a Tuesday it should only have taken a few minutes, but there had been a bomb scare near Oxford Circus, shops had been evacuated, and the traffic tangle caused by police diversions clogged every street. His driver cursed, the taxi crawled its way through the exhaust fumes, and it was after five by the time they drew up outside the office block.

When he got to the third floor, Nancy was the only person in the marine assessors' office. She was putting on her coat, ready to leave.

"Hi." She gave him one of her white-toothed grins, belted the coat loosely around her middle, and reached for her basketwork handbag. "Should I ask if you've had a nice day?"

"I wouldn't recommend it." Laird flopped into a chair, intrigued by the sparkle in her eyes. "What's making you so happy?"

"It's five o'clock, finishing time." She switched to a heavy Jamaican accent. "An dis girl has a real heavy date tonight. How about you, Andrew?"

He shook his head. "Not tonight."

"Well, don't go near any shooting galleries." She was suddenly serious. "I heard about it, and that detective in Dorset was on the phone again. Go carefully, will you?"

"I'll try," he promised.

"Right." She gave him a wink and went out. He heard her singing as she went along the corridor.

He still had to see Osgood Morris, but he wanted to call Sam Harkness first. There were telephone directories on a shelf by the windows, and he located the police number in Poole, dialled it, and asked for the bulky detective inspector's extension.

"Where the hell have you been?" asked Harkness in a peeved growl.

"Out. Earning a living and trying to help us both." Laird jammed the receiver against his shoulder and slouched down in his chair, glad of the telephone line distance that separated them. "Did it matter?"

"It did to some people," said Harkness grimly. "Someone shoots at you, you're supposed to come and tell us—not leave a damn message and disappear." He gave an outraged grunt. "Well, we've got a blue VW van—it may be the one they used, it may not. Stolen in Bournemouth last night, found burned out in a farm lane a couple of hours ago."

"Nothing left behind?"

"Some car tracks, heading away," said Harkness. "Look, can't you give any kind of a description on even one of them?"

"If I could, you'd be first to know," said Laird wryly.

"But you're going to say it has to be linked to Bullen Thoms—right?"

"Unless you've a better idea."

Harkness grunted. "Some people here want proof. They'd be happy to settle for a couple of travelling maniacs out for laughs."

"You mean it happens all the time?" asked Laird sarcastically. "One of your quaint old Dorset customs?"

"Birdshot." Harkness made it an obscenity. "Like hell it happens. But I'm being breathed on, ordered to play it cool. 'Don't frighten the tourist trade, inspector—not when you've nothing solid to go on.'"

"What about the post-mortem?"

"The preliminary report says drowning. The pathology people are still running tests."

"And his briefcase?"

"He could have heaved it into the water. Goodbye foul world of commerce," said Harkness viciously. "God help me, I'm surrounded by high-ranking idiots." He paused and sighed. "We've no evidence, no witnesses—even that damned Rodder woman has decided to fade. She says she needs to get away, that she'll 'keep in touch.' So, unless you've something—"

"Very little," said Laird slowly. There were the diamonds, but that meant stirring trouble, breaking confidences, and did they really help? "He almost certainly brought some papers down with him. He was on some kind of a nervous high—and about the only person he trusted seems to have been Ann Rodder. You got those keys?"

"Yes. You know, one could be for a safe deposit box?"

Laird said nothing.

"Then there's this story she told about Switzerland." A note of suspicion crept into Sam Harkness's voice. "Does that connect at your end?"

"We wish it did," said Laird. "Did you find his passport?"

"No—and nothing in his pockets or on that boat that matters a damn, though we tried again. Hell, I'm getting to know the boat like it was my own." A wistful note crept into Harkness's voice. "Laird, were you ever on tankers?"

"I helped haul a couple off rocks."

"I spent six months on a tanker once, Fleet Auxiliary. They eat well on tankers—sleep well too. Now I've a wife I love but who can't cook, and the phone rings in the middle of every other damned night." Harkness paused. "We still need a statement from you, more than ever now. Suppose I arrange it so you don't have to trail back here?"

"I'd appreciate it," said Laird.

"Tomorrow, then. Meantime, don't talk to any strange men with shotguns," advised Harkness. "They might use buckshot next time —that's another old Dorset custom."

He hung up. Shaking his head, Laird replaced his own receiver and grimaced at the beaming muscle-men pin-ups above the silent, disconnected word processor. One step forward, two steps back—all that seemed to be happening was that the situation was getting messier, more confusing. It seemed a reasonable cue to see Osgood Morris.

He went through to the marine claims manager's office. Morris was at his desk, leaning on his elbows, scowling into space.

"Thinking time?" asked Laird.

"I have a headache. I often have headaches—they go with this job." Osgood Morris sounded strangely tired, even vulnerable for a moment. Then he straightened, his small, narrow face tightened, and he was himself again. "Anything that helps at Thoms's office?"

"Swiss trips and a man's name—Alton."

"At the last count, there were about six and a half million people in Switzerland," said Morris acidly. "Go on."

Laird told him in detail. When he finished, Morris sat silent for a moment, sucking his thin lips.

"Loose ends, but at least they're pointing in the same direction." He sat back. "Alton—it means nothing to me, but we can try a few people. Then there's that damned briefcase. Spoken to your detective friend?"

Laird nodded.

"And?"

"They've got one burned-out van and one half-complete post-mortem. He's struggling."

"Everyone struggles these days," said Morris, unimpressed. "Let's get back to Thoms. I sent Reilly out to that house in Chelsea to use what he calls his Irish charm on the housekeeper. He got in, looked around, but drew a blank. You're seeing him later?"

"He's looking in."

"Then he'll tell you about it. I'll be here for a spell, catching up on a few things." Morris gave a vague gesture of dismissal. "Check with me in the morning."

Osgood Morris waited until Laird had gone. Then, the office door firmly closed, he drew a deep breath and reached for his telephone and dialled a number. He waited, the ringing tone like a hammer in his aching head, and at last it was answered.

"Yes?" The voice was the same as he'd heard before.

"Osgood Morris." He moistened his lips. "Laird has come up with a name—Alton."

"Good," said the voice crisply. "That's what we hoped."

"Couldn't we give him some kind of a hint?" Morris felt sweat on the palms of his hands. "I mean—"

"No." The voice cut him short, politely but firmly. "That was explained, wasn't it?"

"My chairman instructed full co-operation." Morris swallowed. "But—"

"Thank you, Mr. Morris."

The line went dead. His head beginning to pound again, Osgood Morris replaced his receiver. He didn't like anything that was happening now; he wished he could wipe out the last couple of hours and the meetings he had had; he wished above all he'd never heard of Bullen Thoms.

He would take something for this damned headache, then check his one-volume Complete Medical Encyclopaedia. Maybe he was coming down with something.

That way he could stay in bed and say he was sick.

Andrew Laird got to his basement flat soon after six. He'd bought a bottle of Tuscan chianti and a heat-and-eat baked lamb dinner from the little Italian supermarket in Bayswater Road, the only mail lying behind the door was for the absent oilman, and he'd no particular plans for the evening.

Tie loosened, jacket dumped on top of some magazines on a chair, Laird uncorked the chianti, poured a glass, switched the oven on to heat, and thought about going out later. Sipping the wine, he grinned to himself. A lawyer, a tall, dark-haired woman who would have trampled Portia underfoot, had told him once that he was part of a tribe—the rootless ones, the kind who felt lost when they weren't on the move, who didn't have any real kind of life to fall back on.

Two weeks later he'd seen her photograph topping a society gossip column. She'd married an undistinguished politician who certainly had roots—his father owned about a quarter of Wales.

He decided he'd go out for a spell later, drift a little. But the oven was ready. Laird removed the tinfoil wrapping from the lamb dinner, opened the oven, then swore as the telephone began ringing.

He let it keep ringing while he slid the lamb in and nudged the oven shut again, then loped across the room and grabbed the instrument.

"Mr. Laird?" Miguel Holly's voice came cheerfully over the line. "I got your home number from the night man at your office. Are you busy?"

"Not so you'd notice." Laird looked round for the wine. He'd left it just out of reach. "Why?"

"I've a slight problem," said the diamond expert ruefully. "We're supposed to meet tomorrow morning, but I'm not going to be able to make it. Some people want me on a flight to New York—I'm sorry."

"When will you get back?"

"With luck, before the weekend. They think they have a problem —I already know they have," chuckled Holly. "But there's an easy way to solve your Clanmore situation, if you can spare an hour or so."

"Now?" Laird was puzzled. "If we've got to get into that vault again—"

"No, I've made some arrangements," said Holly easily. "I've a workshop on Warris Street, off Leicester Square. Number eleven, top floor—say in about twenty minutes?"

Laird found himself agreeing, with a mental curse at Jerry Reilly for still having the Ford.

He left the oven set at minimum temperature and the chianti bottle on top of the refrigerator, pulled on his jacket, and went out into the early dusk. Fifteen minutes later he came out of the Leicester Square underground station into the lights and crowds, past the cinema posters and the fast-food restaurants, and turned into Warris Street.

It was a small, quiet backwater. The kind of street to be mugged in after dark. A couple of early-shift prostitutes eyed him from a doorway but seemed too lazy to do more about it. He found number eleven, tried the door, and it pushed open.

Laird went in. There was an old-fashioned bird-cage style elevator in the lobby, with gates that clanged shut; then cables quivered, and it rose ponderously once he'd pressed the top-floor button. When the cage stopped, it faced a steel door with a small window. Holly's face appeared, smiled out at him. He heard an automatic lock click; then the elevator gate and door both opened.

"Come in, Mr. Laird." The grey-haired diamond expert closed the steel door as Laird joined him, then led the way along a short corridor into a large room laid out as a combined office and work-shop area. "This won't take too long, I promise you."

Laird glanced at the man, then the room. Miguel Holly was in his shirt sleeves, with a green baize apron tied around his not particularly slender middle. The room, brightly lit, was furnished with an old desk, a couple of work-benches, and an assortment of battered filing cabinets and cupboards. But the laboratory equipment scattered around had cost a small fortune. A few things he could identify—an electron microscope, a sophisticated viewing screen style slide projector, something else that looked like a spectrum analysis unit. But the rest, from racks of precision steel tools and miniature gauges to a machine that might have been a first cousin to a turning lathe, defied him.

"Not a lot, but all I need," said Holly almost apologetically. He tapped his nose. "It's more this than anything—instinct first, checking afterwards."

"Do you work on your own?"

"Always—and anywhere if the price is right." Holly's eyes twinkled behind his spectacles. "As a gemmologist I'm an unusual animal, and that makes me expensive. I had to explain that to Mr. Morris in some detail." He touched Laird's arm and led him over to the nearest work-bench. "Shall we get started?"

Laird blinked. A small square of chamois leather lay on the middle of the bench, eight large diamonds glittering in its middle.

"Are they—?" He glanced at Holly.

Holly nodded.

"I seem to remember Hammerman's Trust wouldn't let them out of their vaults." Laird raised an eyebrow. "How come they changed their minds?"

Holly shrugged. "John Laslow and I go back a long way together. He knows about the New York trip. I've promised the stones will be back with him tonight. Officially—"

"They won't have left?" Laird grinned. "Sounds risky."

"Not as risky as what happened to you, Mr. Laird," said Holly soberly. "That's why I want to help—but tell your friend Morris he'll need to wait till the weekend before he gets anything from me in writing." Leaning over the work-bench, he selected one of the diamonds with a fingertip. "Let's start with this fellow. Know much about diamonds?"

Laird shook his head.

"I'm the sixth generation of our family in this kind of business." Holly crossed to the electron microscope, flicked switches, then got to work. "My great-grandfather mined diamonds in Brazil. My grandfather was tarred and feathered and very nearly hanged in South Africa. Some miners thought he'd cheated them—which he had, except he talked his way out of it." He paused for a moment, peering into the microscope eyepiece, making a careful adjustment. "Everyone knows a diamond is the hardest substance on earth, so those old diamond dealers encouraged the idea that if you hit something that looked like a diamond with a hammer and it broke—well, it wasn't a diamond. Total rubbish. Blame the ancient Romans. They started it."

"And that's what he did?"

"Grandfather?" Holly grunted agreement without looking up. "Hit diamonds with a hammer, and some break, some don't. People destroyed perfectly good diamonds that way for centuries—threw the bits away as rubbish. Grandfather would sit with his little hammer and a block of iron. In would come the miners with their precious stones. Thump, thump with the hammer—sorry, lads, most of these are rubbish, but I'll give you a good price for the rest." He chuckled. "Then the crafty old devil waited till they'd gone, gathered up the debris, and that was more good money in the bank. He'd have been a very rich man, if he hadn't been so fond of roulette wheels."

Humming under his breath, the grey-haired gemmologist rubbed his fingers on the green baize apron, went back to the work-bench, picked up two more of the stones at random, and gave them the same treatment under the microscope. One made him chuckle, but he gave no explanation as he took it and moved across to a small white cabinet fitted with a digital readout, keyboard, and printer. Once the diamond was positioned inside the cabinet, Holly tapped a sequence of instructions on the keyboard.

"My magic box," he explained while the digital readout's lights began flickering. "You'll need a report on spectroscopic analysis, thermal conductivity, and a few other things."

"Will I?"

"Somebody will. Somebody, somewhere always does—eventually," said Holly. "We still like to say the diamond trade is based on trust, that we seal a deal with a handshake. But these days we're up against a lot of crooked technology—damned good synthetic stones, faked stones, altered stones." He tapped his nose again. "Like I said, this comes first—but other people may want more."

"It looks like you can supply it," murmured Laird.

Holly nodded. "I'll give you an example. A diamond should always feel cold to the touch because it has a high thermal conductivity. Measure that, accurately, and it can indicate a stone's quality. But what about the colour? It matters for market value, and colour can be faked—I know a New York cutter, an expert, who lost out that way not long ago. He discovered he'd bought a whole parcel of stones which had been heat-treated."

The printer began chattering softly behind them. Holly waited until it finished, tore off the slip of paper which had emerged, and glanced at it.

"Like some coffee?" he asked. "Then I'll explain what we've got."

A coffee pot was steaming gently on an electric ring beside the desk. Holly produced two mugs and a small carton of milk from one of the desk drawers, and they helped themselves.

"Right." The grey-haired gemmologist perched himself on the edge of his desk and took a first sip of coffee, misting his spectacle lenses in the process. "I'll run a full set of tests on the stones, but I've seen enough to be certain they're all going to be pretty much the same—poor-quality diamonds, faked up, given a face-lift." He shrugged. "That's not illegal, as long as the customer knows what he's buying. If he doesn't, then they're spotted when he tries to sell again. Then he's in for a very nasty surprise."

"Faked up." Laird nursed his coffee mug. "How?"

"There are different ways. With these, I'd say laser treatment and one of the new super-glues." Holly smiled to himself. "Look, a diamond is carbon in very pure but not totally pure form. All kinds of natural inclusions can be caught up in them—things like black carbon spots, seed garnets, minerals. Would you want a diamond that looked sick?"

Laird frowned. "So the laser—"

"Drills a hole down to an impurity, a hole about the diameter of a human hair. Then the inclusion is—well, it can be leached out with acid fumes. But that leaves a little tunnel and a hole at the end, so in goes the super-glue to fill them in." He nodded towards the microscope. "The stones I've checked are riddled like gourmet cheese."

"Expensive cheese." Laird accepted the technicalities behind the simple explanation and took a swallow of coffee. "Anything else you can say about them?"

"They're a mixed bunch—most are probably of South African origin, a couple definitely from Brazil, one might be Indian—that's going on colour and structure."

"A job lot?"

Holly nodded.

"Who would handle that quality of diamond?"

"Untreated?" Holly sighed. "Plenty of dealers, as normal business."

"Treated?"

"You've jumped a step," said the gemmologist. "I told you at the vaults we were dealing with an artist in this field, the best I've come across—ever. There are probably more like these in circulation, but they're the first I've seen." He scratched his chin, open in his interest. "Why do your people think they're from Switzerland?"

"Other reasons. Mainly because Bullen Thoms went out there." Laird saw he couldn't leave it like that. "But we don't know where in Switzerland, except that he used the Zürich airport on the last trip—unless you can make sense of a couple of china cows with ribbon round their necks."

"Ribbon?" Holly raised a bushy eyebrow. "What kind?"

"Ordinary, blue and red striped. Bought in a street market, he told his secretary."

"This market—" Holly spoke softly. "Did he describe it at all?"

Laird shrugged. "Just that it was big enough to get lost in."

Holly sighed and looked smug.

"Then I'll make an intelligent guess," he murmured. "You want Lugano."

Laird stared at him.

"Lugano—or somewhere near. I've worked there. I've holidayed there. You want reasons?" Setting his mug down on the desk, Holly began ticking them off on his fingers. "One, Lugano is in the Ticino, the main Italian-speaking canton of Switzerland. Two, that ribbon—a red and blue stripe is the canton badge, the flag of the Ticino. Three, at Lugano you're only a few minutes drive from the Italian border. Four, step across that border and you're in a village called Luino—which has only one claim to fame. Once a week, every week, it is home to one of the biggest street markets in Europe. I've got lost in it—anyone could." He stopped, chuckled, and eyed Laird almost pityingly. "Any other problems, Laird?"

"Not if you know a man named Alton out there."

"No." Holly shook his head with regret, then hesitated.

"What is it?" Laird waited.

"I didn't think of this before." Holly was still hesitant, almost reluctant. "I have a friend, a relative of sorts, in Lugano. He writes occasionally, usually wanting free advice of some kind. He's a dealer —coins and jewellery, old banknotes, a little of anything." Getting to his feet, he opened one of the desk drawers, rummaged, then tried another. "The damned thing is in here somewhere."

It was a creased, folded cutting from a magazine, a colour photograph of a framed painting, the painting an abstract shirl of pastel shades of yellow and light blue, a winged butterfly trapped large and dark red in the centre. The brief caption beneath was in Italian, and written in ink on the margin were the words *What do you think? B*

"Can I translate?" suggested Holly. "This was a painting shown at a Lugano exhibition last month, in aid of some charity. No artist's name.

"Who's 'B'?"

"Bernardo—Bernardo Garri, my dealer friend." Holly tapped the cutting. "He was right. Do you know what this is?"

"You'd better tell me," said Laird patiently.

"It's a diamond—or at least an artist's impression of a diamond that has been back-lit and magnified. The butterfly"—he shrugged —"a little imagination, perhaps. But I've seen garnet inclusions exactly that colour and near enough that shape."

"A poor-quality stone?"

Holly nodded.

Laird folded the cutting carefully and put it away. "Can we contact him?"

"I will, tomorrow." Holly used a pencil, wrote on a scrap of paper, and passed it over. "But that's the address, a hole-in-a-wall place in the old town." He glanced at his wrist-watch, then towards the work-bench. "I promised John Laslow I wouldn't be too late back with these—"

"I'm going." Laird grinned and gripped his hand. "Thanks. You've helped a lot."

"Or offered you a load of nonsense," said Holly.

"We'll find out." Laird took a first step towards the elevator door, then stopped. "Maybe I should stay till you're finished."

"In case someone knocks me on the head as I leave?" Holly treated the notion mildly. "Mr. Laird, check the directory board in the lobby. This workshop is listed as a dental laboratory. I know the street people, and they know me." He chuckled. "If I'm working late, I'm repairing someone's broken dentures. So don't worry, I'm in no danger."

It was later than he'd intended, close on ten P.M. by the time Andrew Laird got back to the basement flat. He found the baked lamb dinner had become a casualty, even at the oven's low setting, but he managed to scrape away the worst of the charring, salvaged the rest, and washed it down with another glass of chianti.

The late evening news bulletin was on TV. Trouble in the Middle East, trouble in Central America, trouble in Ireland—he let the newscasters drone on for a spell, then killed the sound and let the picture exist in silence. Pouring himself another glass of wine, he took a pen and a few sheets of paper and wrote a brief report on his meeting with Miguel Holly. He could knock it into final shape in the morning, when he got to the Clanmore office.

Finished, he read the sheets through again and was still frowning at the last one when the telephone began ringing. Reaching over, Laird lifted the receiver and answered, trying to keep the yawn out of his voice.

The caller was Osgood Morris. He sounded very much on edge.

"Where have you been?" asked the marine claims manager, his

high-pitched voice shrill on the line. "This is the third time I've tried—"

"I was out. Your diamond expert wanted to see me."

"And now you're waiting on Jerry Reilly?"

"He'll be here, sometime." Laird glanced at his wrist-watch and grinned. He couldn't imagine the Irishman arriving until well after midnight. "Why?"

"Reilly is in the hospital. He's had emergency surgery. He'll live, but he's still in intensive care," said Morris. "I'd call it mistaken identity—it was meant to be you."

"Me?" Laird felt a moment's cold sickness, then bewilderment. "What the hell happened, Osgood? He had the car; he was going to meet some girl—"

"In Knightsbridge. She was at her window, waiting, and saw it happen." Morris spoke quickly, as if wanting to get it over. "Reilly got there about seven-thirty, stopped across the street from her place, left the car, started to cross the street, and a black Jaguar car, two men aboard, came out of nowhere and ran him down. It didn't stop, but the girl managed to catch the licence number."

"How bad is he?"

"I told you, he's had surgery. He was thrown about twenty feet— a broken femur, internal injuries, a broken shoulder, concussion." Morris made it a catalogue. "The police found his identification, then contacted me."

Laird swore bitterly. "And the thugs in the Jaguar?"

"They weren't particularly lucky." Morris didn't hide his satisfaction. "The car was spotted about twenty minutes later, on the north circular route, and was chased. The damn fool driving it lost control at about eighty and hit a lamp standard—both men aboard were killed instantly. The police found an automatic pistol and a sawn-off shotgun in among the wreckage."

"So they were my two?"

"It looks that way."

"What about names?"

"One had a French passport which says he was Henri Lasay and an airline ticket stub which says he flew from Paris to Heathrow yesterday. There's nothing certain about the driver—the lamp standard made that difficult." Morris paused for a moment; then Laird heard a sound close to a sigh. "Put it together. Reilly hasn't anything troublesome on his current workload; he has only been on the fringe of the Thoms affair. At night, under street lights—well, there's a superficial likeness to you."

Laird didn't answer. But there might be.

"So if this pair discovered they hadn't particularly damaged you this afternoon, they'd be disappointed," Morris suggested. "Suppose they watched the Clanmore entrance later. They'd see Reilly driving out in the car you'd been using. Maybe they saw him going over to Thoms's house. Then, if they stuck with him—"

All they had to do was wait, until their chance came. Laird drew a deep breath. If Jerry Reilly hadn't agreed to take the Ford and have the smashed windshield replaced, he could have been the one in that hospital bed.

"When will we know more about Jerry?" he asked.

"The doctors say tomorrow—late tomorrow, and no visitors till after that. I've been at the hospital, with the police, but was turned away." Morris brightened. "Well, presuming these two came over to —ah—dispose of Bullen Thoms, then make some kind of arrangement as far as you were concerned, at least that's finished. But why did you have to see Holly?"

"He has to go to New York, so he ran the diamond tests tonight," said Laird wearily. "They confirmed what he'd told us."

"At the fee he charges, I'll want that in detail," sniffed Morris. "Anything else?"

"He says Bullen Thoms probably went to Lugano."

"Lugano?" The marine claims manager made it a squeak. "Why?"

Laird told him. After a moment, Morris made a nervous, throat-clearing noise.

"It sounds—well, possible. Do you think he's right?"

"I'd prefer your word—possible."

"Lugano." Morris was thinking. "Yes, in fact it could—" he stopped. "We can work on it tomorrow. There's not much we could do tonight. Just don't trouble the hospital people—they'll call me if there's any change."

The line went dead. Laird sat for several moments, eyes closed, then gently replaced his receiver.

It had to have been the way Morris had said, but why? It was the same question he'd kept asking himself since that moment when that shotgun had blasted at him from the blue Volkswagen van—and suddenly a possible, chilling answer had struck him.

Bullen Thoms had gone off to Switzerland, seeking a way out of the Clanmore trap. Suppose, instead of admitting what had happened, he'd thought it wiser, safer, to claim he was being blackmailed—that someone could expose him, destroy his front of being a respected shipbroker.

Laird chewed his lower lip, frowning, following it through.

If Thoms had named Andrew Laird as his fictitious blackmailer, if the people he'd hoped would help had decided instead that Thoms was less of a risk dead, then it was a small step from there to deciding that the blackmailer should also be put out of circulation. Leaving everything neat and tidy, from their viewpoint.

Except that it had shaped into something very different.

To hell with Osgood Morris's advice. He lifted the phone and quickly dialled the Middlesex Hospital number.

All hospital switchboard operators seemed to be picked for their ability to sound blandly reassuring.

The one at the Middlesex was no exception.

"The ward report on Mr. Reilly says he is fairly comfortable," she told him.

Laird thanked her, hung up, and wondered if Jerry Reilly would have agreed.

CHAPTER FOUR

"Cops," said the commissionaire on the front door of the Clanmore Alliance building. He gave the warning out of the corner of his mouth. "Three of 'em, Mr. Laird. To see you."

Then the man ambled off across the lobby, beaming at the rest of the early morning world.

Andrew Laird had expected it. But at least there had been no overnight change in Jerry Reilly's condition. He'd phoned again the moment he'd wakened, and the hospital bulletin was still the same.

The police reception committee was waiting for him when he got to the third floor and the marine assessors' room. They were expecting him—the commissionaire, a man of tight-rope abilities, must have phoned up. Osgood Morris was with them, along with a bland-faced man from Clanmore's legal department. Anyone else around had been cleared from the room.

"I'm Detective Inspector Edwards, Mr. Laird." The oldest of the police trio, a thin man with a small moustache and very little hair, gave a moderately friendly nod. "Early in today, aren't you?"

Laird glanced at the clock on the wall. It showed a few minutes after nine.

"I—ah—explained to Inspector Edwards that we often work fairly flexible hours," said Morris hastily. He gave a quick, eager smile, ignoring the legal department man's frown. "Claims people don't have a regular routine."

"But I decided we'd wait anyway," said Edwards. He turned back to Laird, indicating his companions. "Sergeant Croft and Sergeant Lands—Lands is from Traffic Branch, just sitting on the sidelines because of last night."

Croft was a burly, fair-haired man wearing a leather jacket and corduroys. Lands was in uniform, with a long service medal ribbon on his tunic. Both considered Laird with a mild degree of interest but said nothing.

"You can guess the main reason we're here. There's a request in from Poole C.I.D. asking us to get a statement from you, and one from your boss." Edwards paused and sucked his lips, his long, thin face giving away very little. "It seems you both beat us to it."

"We try," said Laird. The legal department man, standing behind the three policemen, gave a slight, fractional nod which didn't need translation. "But any way I can help—"

"I've given Inspector—ah—Edwards a copy of that draft statement you prepared," said Osgood Morris. "You'll remember, Andrew, I said it would be a good idea." He beamed hopefully at the detective. "Any time we can, Clanmore likes to co-operate."

The legal department man made a suitable noise of agreement. His eyes were still on Laird; the message remained clear.

"I've read it." Edwards crooked a finger at his sergeant. Reaching into his leather jacket, the sergeant drew out an envelope and handed it over. Opening the envelope, taking out the folded typewritten sheets inside, Edwards glanced at Laird. "Want to see it again?"

"I'd better," agreed Laird.

"Right." Edwards switched his attention to Osgood Morris and the legal department man. "No need for you two to wait. Sergeant—"

His sergeant shepherded both men out of the room before they could protest. Once they'd gone, he closed the door firmly and leaned against it with a wisp of a grin. The Traffic Branch sergeant had drifted over to a window and was making a pretence at being interested in the view.

"You know what I think of this?" Edwards laid the statement on the nearest desk. "Nice, concise, and sanitised—all your own work?"

"We write a lot of reports," said Laird gravely.

Edwards swore softly but pungently and moved away. Drawing up a chair, Laird sat down and began reading.

Osgood Morris and the legal department had been busy. The statement he had allegedly composed was a careful blend of truth, delicately couched phrasing, and selective omissions. They'd drawn from his own taped reports, the Clanmore files, and his conversations with Osgood Morris, then diluted them further wherever necessary before stirring everything together with a legal department flourish. They had covered his meeing with Bullen Thoms, his second visit to Poole, the shotgun attack on his return trip to London.

But not the rest.

He turned over the last sheet, looked up, and met Edwards's gaze.

"That's the way I'd tell it, Inspector."

"And there's probably another version, set to music," said the thin-faced detective. He produced his cigarette and lit one with a match, breaking the match carefully before dropping it into an ashtray. "Nothing you want to change?"

Laird shook his head.

"Now there's a surprise," said Edwards's sergeant, still at the door. He scowled. "I think—"

"Don't," said Edwards wearily.

The sergeant blinked. "But—"

"No." Edwards leaned on the edge of the desk and sighed. "Laird, someone seems to think you're a friend—this cop Sam Harkness at Poole. He wants you to call him. Just one thing first, for the sake of our Traffic Branch friend"—he paused and raised his voice—"if you're listening, Sergeant Lands."

"Sir." The man glanced round from his window, grinned, and nodded.

"According to your boss, you got back here, you gave your car keys to this Jerry Reilly, and Reilly said he'd have the windscreen fixed." Edwards drew on his cigarette and let the smoke out in a slow trickle. "Did you see him, hear from him, after that?"

"No." Laird shook his head.

"That's what he said—he was conscious for a few minutes before they operated on him last night." Edwards gave Laird a slight smile. "I tried to see him this morning, but a pocket-sized nurse threw me out. No one gets near him till tomorrow, but you know how it goes with the Irish—they bounce back. He'll be all right."

"What about the two who died in the Jaguar?"

"You know about the Frenchman?" Edwards accepted Laird's nod. "The other was home-grown—we identified him on a fingerprint check, because he wasn't left very pretty. Jimbo Adair—Sebastian on his birth certificate. He was London based, a fairly high-priced hired muscle and driver, one of the brighter ones. Strictly free-lance."

"That's all?" Laird felt the same dull rage flooding in again. "No leads back?"

"Not in that league." Edwards shook his head. "Make your call."

Conscious that his audience wasn't going to go away, Laird used the nearest telephone. A few seconds later, Sam Harkness was on the other end of the line.

"I know about last night," said Harkness with gruff sympathy. "Hard luck on your mate—but that's not why I wanted to talk."

"If it's the statement—" began Laird.

"No. I'll get it soon enough. But I promised I'd tell you how things went down here." Harkness broke off to mutter to someone at his end, then picked up where he'd left off. "I've the Bullen Thoms autopsy report in front of me. He drowned, no doubt about it. All the signs are there, and the chloride content of the blood is way up."

"How high?"

"The pathologist says more than thirty per cent. You follow?"

"Yes." Laird's mouth tightened. Drown in fresh water, and water in the lungs lowered the chloride content of blood. Drown in salt water, and the chloride level could increase up to forty per cent. "So he was alive when he went in?"

"Unless something really weird happened." Harkness gave a humourless chuckle. "Even weirder than what we've got—there's more, because the lab people knew I was twitchy. He'd been drinking, and there was liquor in the stomach, but they also came up with traces of chloral hydrate."

Laird swore under his breath. It was a complete, unexpected turnaround. Chloral hydrate, the old-fashioned knockout, still legitimately used to treat mental and nervous conditions, was tasteless in alcohol and could act like a stupefying bomb. A few drops could mug the central nervous system and reduce a victim to a state of collapse in minutes. He'd sleep it off, unless it was overdone.

"What else did they say?" he asked sharply.

"Enough, even for my boss," said Harkness. "We're talking murder, not suicide. What I have to do is tie in those two nasties who got wiped out last night."

"Yes." Laird glanced round. Edwards was watching him; his sergeant and the Traffic man were both hovering near, and he saw their faces. They already knew; they had gone through the kind of pre-arranged ritual demanded when two separate police forces found themselves sharing the same situation. "Sam? Can you—tie them in, I mean?"

"Not yet," admitted Harkness. "And I wondered about the woman—Ann Rodder. But time of death is estimated at around two a.m.; we've got a witness who saw him alone, heading back to his own boat from the *Lady Ann* half an hour earlier. More important, one of the marina staff says a man quizzed him about vacant berths that afternoon, then said he knew Bullen Thoms and wanted to know where Thoms kept his boat."

"Any description?"

"Hazy." Laird could almost hear Harkness shrug. "He was busy; there were other people around—you know how it goes."

Bullen Thoms had had visitors waiting, visitors with a cold-blooded task ahead. But, afterwards, they had been somewhere near when daylight came. Watching, waiting again, Laird felt a momentary chill. He hadn't fully thought of it before, but Bullen Thoms must have told them he was going to turn up.

"This chloral hydrate stuff"—Harkness wasn't finished—"the pathology mob say it means Thoms couldn't have tied as much as a daisy chain round his neck."

"Or got along that deck," agreed Laird. "Do you stop there?"

"You mean what about who sent them?" Harkness asked. "There's a public relations answer to that—the file stays open. But from the way you told things when you were here, I wouldn't bet on anything." He paused. "We've still that damned safe deposit key and a few other puzzles, but my boss doesn't want to know. So—do me a favour?"

"Name it," said Laird.

"Stay away from here—unless it's after working hours."

They said goodbye and Laird hung up. Turning, he faced Edwards again. The Metropolitan detective made a gesture which wasn't totally apologetic.

"No surprises?"

Laird shook his head.

"But now you know the score." Edwards pointed at the typewritten pages on the desk. "Want to change any of that?"

"Not particularly." Laird brought out his pen and scribbled his signature on the last page.

"Tell your scriptwriter I like his style," said Edwards acidly while his sergeant gathered up the sheets. "I don't buy this, Laird. If it was totally my case—" He stopped. "We'll be back. You understand?"

Laird nodded.

"Right." Edwards signalled the two sergeants that it was time to leave. "At least I'm going to give your boss a few unpleasant moments before we go, whoever his friends may be."

"You've got my blessing on that," Laird told him.

The detective looked at him for a moment, and the man's face thawed a little.

"Whatever it is that's going on, good luck," he said in a more friendly voice. "If he's a sample, you'll need it."

"Up the workers," said Laird, and watched them go out.

It was another ninety minutes before he got to see Osgood Morris. The marine claims manager was busy, not to be disturbed for any reason, according to his secretary. The police team accounted for maybe twenty minutes of that time but no more. Laird could only wait while a tearful Nancy offered him cups of coffee and a succession of people from other departments found some excuse to look in, make sympathetic noises about Jerry Reilly, then try to find out what was going on.

He phoned the hospital again. Their bulletin had changed, Reilly was described as "making progress."

Nancy burst into tears again, then made more coffee.

At last the summons came, and he went along the corridor to Osgood Morris's office. The marine claims manager looked flushed, slightly agitated, but still pleased with himself. He waved Laird into a chair, and waited until he had settled.

"You—ah—probably feel I owe you an apology." His smile across the desk had a nervous edge. "That statement, I mean. I meant to warn you, but—"

"I signed it."

"Yes." Morris gave an indignant sniff. "Detective Inspector Edwards—ah—discussed that with me." He put the memory behind him, except for one aspect. "At least we know for sure now about Bullen Thoms. That autopsy report—unpleasant."

"He wouldn't know much about it." Laird leaned on his side of the desk. "Osgood, whose idea was that piece of fiction I was supposed to have written?"

"I took advice." Morris's eyes flickered briefly towards the ceiling. "There's been discussion, some decisions—for instance, we're dropping a strong hint about those diamonds, to the right people."

"Did anyone decide what we do next?" asked Laird sarcastically. "Or do we just back off?"

"Now?" Morris stiffened in surprise. "We've our own interests to protect, Andrew. Thoms dead, one of the staff in the hospital, you damned nearly there ahead of him—"

"You really mean you still want to know what Bullen Thoms intended to trade?" said Laird.

Morris hesitated, pursed his lips, then nodded.

"There's a possibility. It seems Thoms began putting out feelers about three months ago—indirect feelers, not in his own name. He wanted to arrange a time charter of two, perhaps three medium-sized cargo ships. From a Mediterranean port if possible—"

"What kind of time charter?"

"Dry hull."

Laird shaped an involuntary whistle. Dry hull meant just that—only the ship was chartered, the people paying the bill supplying their own crew, going where they wanted, the cargo their concern and no one else involved.

"Did he fix a deal?"

"I don't know," admitted Morris. "That's all my—ah—source had available."

"Trust him?"

"He gave me the first hint Thoms was behind the coffee fraud. We've had other dealings."

"To mutual advantage?" Laird shrugged. Every insurance company had funds for that kind of situation and used them. But two, maybe three ships—he could understand Morris's alarm, the whole marine insurance industry's concern. Any one of these ships could be like a ticking timebomb of a future Insured Risk claim totalling millions.

"These ships—there's no way we can narrow it down. You know that." Morris clasped his hands together and scowled at his knuckles. "We're talking about thousands of shipping movements. What does the insurance community do, suspend all business?"

Laird shrugged. He couldn't argue because Morris was right. Clanmore itself might even be involved already, either directly or because it had taken a share of someone else's business in the same way as the betting industry laid off heavy stakes.

"We've got to find out our own way," emphasised Morris. He bared his teeth in one of his weasel grins. "That's why I'm sending you to Switzerland."

"Lugano?" Laird had seen it coming.

"Lugano. I telephoned Miguel Holly last night, after you told me. I went over things with him." Morris was pleased with himself now, and his squeaky voice showed it. "The man is an oddity, but he talked reasonable sense—and he agreed to contact his friend there, say you were coming. You're booked on an afternoon flight."

"Thanks for telling me," said Laird. He considered the marine claims manager through narrowed eyes. "It's not just Holly. You've got more, haven't you?"

"Yes." Morris gave an irritating smirk. "I explored a possibility and it paid off. When Thoms flew to Zürich last weekend, he paid by credit card and the airline concerned—ah—obliged by giving us his card number from their records. Luckily we've a reasonable relationship with most of the plastic money people, so when we gave them the card number they made a computer scan through their records." He shook his head. "Too early, of course, to know if he made any other credit purchases on that trip—if he did, it will still take time for the vouchers to be fed back here and be processed. But they did turn up items from some previous trips—hotel, car hire, bits and pieces."

"Lugano?"

"Almost all of them. You'll have a list."

Laird hid the way he felt. The mutual aid club had been at work again, outpacing any legal system. From cradle to grave, almost everyone was recorded somewhere in more ways than they could ever guess. Credit cards and credit ratings were mere extensions.

But there was another possibility.

"How does your Mafia relate with gnomes?"

"Gnomes?" Morris blinked. "You mean did he have a Swiss bank account?" He shook his head. "With the Swiss, that's talking religion. We didn't even try—we'd have been wasting time."

"Then what about that name his secretary gave me?" demanded Laird. "Alton—you were going to work on it."

"I did. It doesn't stir anyone's memory." Glancing at his watch, Morris got to his feet. "Do what you can. I'll stay in touch. Did you know we were flying young Reilly's parents in from Dublin?"

"No." Laird rose, the meeting pointedly over. "Are they staying?"

"Till he's on the mend." Morris grimaced. "Hopefully that won't be too long—we're having to put them up in a hotel. Right, anything you need will be on your desk."

Laird nodded and went towards the door.

"One more thing," said Morris hastily, "stay out of trouble. I'd rather pull you out than—well, you understand?"

"Stay out of trouble," agreed Laird. The warning made him smile. "You sound like you've been dipping into the pension fund."

Osgood Morris waited until the door had closed, then any pretence at a smile left his lips. He swallowed hard.

He didn't like it. He didn't like it at all, and he had to telephone that number again.

But at least the chairman had invited him out for lunch.

The afternoon Swissair flight from Heathrow to Zürich, a DC-9, left Terminal Two exactly on time and climbed quickly through heavy clouds into the sunlight. The passenger load was light, there were plenty of empty seats, and the blue-uniformed stewardesses managed to bring the bar trolley round both before and after the anonymous meal they served.

Swissair cutlery was high quality. Gaunt watched a tubby, sober-suited businessman in an aisle seat two rows in front make a quick, surreptitious job of stealing a knife and spoon, slipping them into his jacket pocket. The stewardess said nothing when she collected the man's meal tray, but she had noticed. She came back a little later, smiled gently, and solemnly placed a clean fork in front of him.

Swissair girls were well trained.

As the stewardess walked towards the rear of the aircraft, the tubby cutlery stealer turned and glared at her back. Then his eyes met Laird's. He flushed and stiffened as if realising there had been a witness to his little crime, then made a feeble attempt at an embarrassed grin, and shrank back into his seat.

By then, the DC-9 was beginning to lose height. A tail wind had cut five minutes off the scheduled flight time of one hour thirty-five minutes, and they came down through another blanket of cloud into a grey view of Zürich airport with the city of Zürich and its long, narrow lake a vague haze to the south.

They landed smoothly, the DC-9's passengers were shepherded into the customs hall, and although there was a twenty-minute delay before any luggage appeared on the baggage carousel, customs and immigration checks after that amounted to a walk-through formality. Carrying his travel bag, Andrew Laird followed the others into the main terminal building.

The tubby man who stole cutlery was in front of him, hurrying, carrying a small leather overnight case. But Laird lost sight of him almost immediately in the crowded bustle. Zürich's airport terminal wasn't so much a building as a multi-storey shopping and business centre constructed round a central plaza, a tourist-trap maze of brightly lit levels swarming with people, crammed with booths and kiosks. Museum piece single-seat aircraft dangled by wires from ceilings, crammed escalators purred, busy restaurants and snack bars had queues waiting for service.

Laird stopped outside a shop offering a window display of Swiss costume dolls and wrist watches, put down his travel bag, and got his bearings. The Clanmore Alliance travel department had booked him through by train from Zürich to Lugano, with the explanation that Lugano had only a local airstrip for light aircraft. He was scheduled to take the airport rail-link into Zürich Central, then join an inter-city express train south. It stopped at Lugano before it went on to Milan in Italy.

He spotted rail-link signs in several languages over a broad archway two floors down and at the same time saw the tubby man again.

He was near the archway, at a rendezvous point sign, talking to a thin, dark-haired stranger dressed in black. They stopped. Both looked around; then the stranger headed off at a lope towards a line of public telephones. The tubby man disappeared from sight as a package-tour group of travellers were herded past by a courier waving a large clipboard.

Laird shrugged, checked his watch against a large timepiece ticking in the centre of the shop-window display, then headed down. When he reached the rail-link archway, another escalator took him down yet another level to the station platform.

A train had just pulled out. He waited while the platform gradually filled up again, the people around him a mixture of tourists and local Swiss, more and more arriving until the platform was jammed with people and luggage. Warning lights flashed, a metallic Swiss-German voice rasped from the public address system overhead, and the next train purred into sight. The crowd pressed forward, pushing him nearer the edge of the platform. A group of youngsters laden with climbing gear raised a cheer.

Pulled by a large, olive-green locomotive, the train came rumbling in. Then it happened. Someone shoved hard against Laird and a hand seized him by the arm. He tried to turn; another shove took him to the lip of the platform. He saw the tubby man beside him in the crowd, saw the glitter in the man's eyes—then those same eyes suddenly showed horror, the lips twisted in terror, and the tubby man was falling. A woman screamed. The tubby man landed on the track, then disappeared under the slowing locomotive.

Brakes squealed, the same woman kept screaming, other people were shouting. About half a coach length went past before the rail-link train shuddered to a halt. Then everything was suddenly quiet; even the screaming had stopped. Some railwaymen and a couple of uniformed police pushed their way through and disappeared under the carriages.

Shaken, his mouth dry, Laird stood with his back to the stationary coach. One of the policemen emerged again, looked up at a waiting porter, and shook his head. Another railwayman crawled back out on the platform near Laird and was noisily sick. The tubby man's leather case lay between them, burst open, its contents scattered.

"*Bitte.*" A worried-looking station official came over. "*Sind Sie unverletzt?*" He saw Laird hesitate and tried again. "English?"

Laird nodded.

"Are you all right?"

"Yes." Laird drew a deep breath. "Yes, I am." He glanced along the coach. "Is he dead?"

"*Ja.*" The railwayman had grey hair and a sympathetic face. "This man—did you know him, did you see what happened?"

"No." It was near enough the truth. Had he seen anything, had the man said anything? Laird wasn't sure.

"*Danke.*" The railwayman sighed and glanced back at the other spectators. "So many damn people, and nobody seems to know anything."

He turned away to talk to one of the policemen. The platform around was emptying, the crowd melting away in the direction of another train while the metallic voice began grating from the loudspeakers with another unemotional announcement.

Laird stood back, drew a deep breath, and saw the ashen-faced young porter who had vomited. He had begun the slow, half-hearted task of collecting the spilled, widely scattered contents of the leather case, and some were lying near Laird's feet. Stooping, Laird bent to help. He picked up an electric razor and some handkerchiefs, gave them to the porter, then stooped again.

The dead man had had a British passport. Lifting it, Laird flicked the pages, saw the name David Trimble and the occupation "salesman," then saw something loose protruding from the next page. He drew it out, then froze.

He was staring at his own photograph. It was a head and shoulders, with the kind of out-of-focus background which meant a telephoto lens. But it was a street just outside the Clanmore building.

Laird slipped the photograph into his jacket pocket, closed the passport, and laid it back where he'd found it. The porter hadn't noticed. He was puzzling over a torn paper napkin, wrapped round the stolen Swissair cutlery.

The other railwaymen and the two policemen were in a huddle at the platform's edge. More railwaymen were coming, carrying a stretcher. Picking up his travel bag, Laird quietly eased away, boarded the other rail-link train, and took a seat on the far side. A few minutes later the doors closed and the shuttle train moved off. Laird had a last glimpse of the men on the platform; then the rail-link plunged into a long, black tunnel.

In another fifteen minutes they pulled into Zürich Central, near the heart of the Swiss city. The long line of C.N.R. coaches which made up the international Lugano–Milan express was already murmuring at the next platform, ready to leave.

Laird boarded it straight away, walked most of its length through coaches where red upholstery signified smoking areas and green upholstery non-smoking territory, and finally settled in one of an empty group of seats close to the front. He had his back to a partition, a clear view of the platform, and he kept his travel bag at his feet. He scanned the other passengers coming aboard, most of them family groups who chattered happily in Italian as if the train had already ceased to be in Swiss-German territory.

No police appeared; the only uniforms belonged to railway porters. He wasn't sure who he was watching for or why; the only face in his mind was that of the tubby man who had died under the rail-link's locomotive.

A last bustle happened along the platform. Then, gently, the Lugano–Milan express began gliding out of the station. In a few minutes it was travelling along the southern edge of the Zürichsee, the lake's placid water sprinkled with small craft, some of the city's outer suburbs a peaceful sprawl on the opposite bank.

Two nuns who had boarded late were sitting a few seats away, gossiping quietly. One laughed. She had a round, cheerful face and clutched a shopping basket. Suddenly Laird felt the tension inside him drawing away leaving him oddly empty inside, clear-headed, able to relax and think.

Taking the photograph from his pocket, he cupped it in his hand. It was recent, very recent, probably taken within the last couple of days. He could be certain of that much from the way he was dressed.

So someone had managed a fast printing job. But why had the tubby man been carrying it? Frowning to himself, Laird tried to recall every small detail of those few moments at the airport's rail-link station.

What had happened, why had it happened? The tubby man had

intended to kill him—or had he? If that had been the intention, what had gone wrong?

An accident, the railway official had said. There had been that surge forward; no one in the crowd had seen anything. Trying hard, Laird couldn't remember anything that helped except the sudden look of terror on that fat face.

Who else had been near them? That was another blank in those few chaotic seconds.

He sighed and looked again at the photograph. The tubby man had been carrying it and had been on the same flight from London. He'd talked briefly to the dark-haired man at Zürich airport—then the dark-haired man had vanished.

Laird caught a glimpse of his own craggy face, a reflection in the window glass across the compartment, and glared at it in frustration.

Someone had to have realised the wrong man had been run down in London. The same someone must have arranged for the tubby man to follow him, to board that Swissair flight for Zürich.

But after that? He felt certain the tubby man had meant to kill him. Yet now the man was dead, and he was still alive. Had it really been an accident, a wry twist of fate?

The train clattered briskly over a set of points and brought him back to his surroundings. The nun with the shopping basket gave him a friendly smile and Laird smiled back at her.

He'd find out most things eventually, probably the hard way. Settling back in his seat, he suddenly realised he was humming to himself. The tune was an old Beatles number.

Things weren't too bad yet.

The scenery changed. Around Zürich it had been level, with a few low hills. But it was a three and a half hour journey to the Ticino, and as dusk closed in they reached the first of the mountains. Small, shingle-roofed chalets clung to the lower slopes, sheer rock faces rose above then were lost in the clouds. Sometimes a mountain stream poured a milky grey torrent down into a valley where cars moved like toys.

Dusk had already given way to darkness by the time the train plunged and rocked into the long claustrophobic night of the St. Gotthard tunnel. Laird dozed, lost count of distance, then came awake again with a start as a bright white flash seemed to sear through his eyelids.

They were in the open again, south of the tunnel, high up, rain slashing against the coach windows, a thunderstorm raging outside. Sheet lightning danced and shivered between mountains, showing them in brief, stark clarity before they vanished in blackness again, each thunder peal seeming to shake train and track. A child was crying further down the coach; one of the nuns looked distinctly unhappy.

The storm stayed with them without any sign of easing. But at last the train gradually began to brake, rounded a long curve, and the lights of a large town appeared far below with a dull glint of lake in the background.

"*Sì, signore*, Lugano." The round-faced nun beamed an answer to his unspoken question, then nudged her half-asleep companion and began packing their picnic basket, humming to herself.

Laird peered again at the lights and the lake. There was little to see, but he remembered the maps he had studied. Somewhere over there the Swiss-Italian frontier ran like a jagged edge with pockets of both nations side by side. He sighed, and the window glass steamed up. Geography was just one more problem to add to the rest.

A few minutes later the train rumbled into Lugano station and drew to a halt. The rain was still falling, and there was general confusion on the platform as travellers left the coaches and others who had been waiting tried to get aboard.

Laird eased his way through the noisy bustle, reached a line of waiting taxis, and threw his bag aboard the nearest. Clanmore's travel department had booked him into the Hotel Orchidea, the same hotel that had featured in Bullen Thoms's credit-card statements, and the taxi driver got him there in a matter of minutes through rain-soaked streets where anything with wheels threw up a bow-wave of spray.

The Orchidea was an old, stone-fronted building near the centre of town, facing the lakeside, separated from it by a broad, busy road. Paying the driver, picking up his bag again, Andrew Laird grimaced to himself. Clanmore's travel department, always budget conscious, had a gift for selecting elderly, worn-out hotels and would have approved of Bullen Thoms's choice. Traces of faded glory showed in wrought ironwork balconies, window shutters, and the crumbling archway above the main door.

He went in. The lobby was panelled in wood; an old woman dozed in one of the armchairs with an ancient dog curled comfortably at her feet. At the reception desk, the night clerk was a fat, middle-aged man in shirt sleeves and an open waistcoat. He had a telephone at his ear and was frowning at a chessboard.

"Buon giorno." Laird coaxed his rusty Italian to life after a moment or two. "I have a reservation."

"Signore." The night clerk looked up, startled, gave a brief welcoming nod, moistened his lips, then carefully moved one of the chess pieces. He spoke briefly into the phone, then laid it down beside him and gave an apologetic grin. "Your name, *signore?*"

Laird registered, and the man laid a room key in front of him.

"Prego . . . and there was a telephone message for you, from Signor Garri. He looks forward to seeing you tomorrow morning." The chubby face needed a shave but showed a friendly curiosity. "You are a collector, Signor Laird?"

"In a small way," lied Laird. "You know Bernardo Garri?"

"Everyone in Lugano knows him." The night clerk gave an expansive grin. "A good man, a fair man—though sometimes he bellows like a bull. What is it you collect, *signore?* Coins, medals, old silver, maybe?"

"Anything that doesn't cost too much." Laird took the key. "Any other messages for me?"

The night clerk shook his head then glanced sideways at the waiting chessboard. "Do you play chess, *signore?*"

Laird looked at the board and remembered a drunken Welsh ship's engineer who had taught him just how little he knew about the game during one long Pacific trip. The night clerk was playing a variation on what the Welshman had called a Casablanca game, no territory for amateurs.

"You're way ahead of my league," he told the night clerk. "Who have you got on the other end of the phone?"

"My brother—he is night operator at the *polizia* switchboard." The man sighed. "He says he is four moves off checkmate."

"Four?" A faint memory stirred as Laird looked at the pieces again. "You've an unemployed knight. Why not bring on the cavalry?"

The night clerk blinked, swore, and turned back to the board. A new sound had begun behind them. The old lady in the armchair was snoring.

Laird's room was on the second floor. He walked up, found his door at the end of a short, poorly lit corridor, and went in.

It was a reasonable-sized room, spotlessly clean, simply furnished, with a small bathroom located behind a folding door. He had a window and narrow balcony overlooking the lake, the rain still pattering on the glass, traffic swishing along the road below. The bed was big and felt comfortable, and a basket of fruit, apples and pears, lay on the dressing table.

Maybe Bullen Thoms hadn't picked too badly.

Laird unpacked, washed, then frowned at the telephone at the bedside. He was tempted to get word back to Osgood Morris about what had happened at Zürich. But he thought about it again and shook his head. It could wait till morning.

The Orchidea's bar and restaurant were on the ground floor, both moderately busy, the custom a mixture of foreign tourists and elderly dowager females, the latter looking and acting like permanent residents. He ordered a whisky at the bar, drank it slowly while he amused himself by looking at the mural of Swiss mountain-climbing which covered every wall, then went through to the restaurant. He ate by himself at a corner table, his main course a grilled veal dish served with a thick cream sauce, his nearest neighbours a young couple who spoke French and who held hands every moment they could.

By the time he'd finished eating, the view from the restaurant showed that the rain had stopped. It was a few minutes after ten, and he felt in a walking mood. Going back to his room, Laird collected his coat, locked the door behind him as he left, and went down to the hotel lobby.

The night clerk was dealing with a new arrival. An attractive, dark-haired woman in her late twenties, she was talking to him, while he smiled and nodded vigorous, happy agreement. Her luggage, two small canvas suitcases, was on the floor beside her.

They were both too busy to notice as Laird went past. But she was medium height, wearing a white sweater and dark trousers with high-heeled boots, and had a three-quarter-length leather coat hanging loosely from her shoulders. He caught a sideways glimpse of her firmly boned face and smiling mouth, and heard her laugh at something the night clerk said.

Laird went outside. A white Opel coupe with mud-spattered Zürich number-plates was parked at the hotel door, empty, the exhaust still crackling as it cooled in the damp.

If the Orchidea's new guest had come from Zürich, she'd driven a long way. Laird looked back into the hotel, smiled to himself, then set off.

The rain clouds had cleared, Lugano had shaken itself after the downpour. The town was coming back to life again under a star-lit sky; the moon glinted on the mirror-smooth water of her lake with its edge of black hills and distant mountains.

The pavements were busy and cheerfully noisy. People window-shopped outside brightly lit jewellery stores and fashion houses, branches of some of the top names in Europe. Others were beginning to pack the pavement café tables as fast as waiters could wipe things dry. The main road and every side road carried a constant flow of traffic, from sleek Rolls-Royce limousines to rasping little motor scooters. Every other corner seemed to be occupied by a bank building crowned by a neon sign; every other doorway seemed to be topped by a large Swiss flag and a matching red and blue Ticino canton banner.

There was money in Lugano, a lot of money. It showed in the shop window displays; it showed in the fashionably dressed women being escorted into hotels, in the lines of powerboats moored along the lakeside, in the low-key but ubiquitous police presence. Standing at the kerb, Laird watched a two-man patrol go past. They strolled along in their smartly tailored blue uniforms, each with a baton bumping gently at his hip, a pistol holstered at his waist, and reached a rowdy group of teenagers gathered round a cluster of parked motor cycles. Both men stayed smiling, toughly competent. They said a few words, and suddenly the group had melted away, climbing on their machines and setting off in different directions.

The two policemen strolled on again, and Laird used a gap in the flow of traffic to cross the main road to the lakeside walkway. He was near a scatter of water-bus piers, boats loading at two of them. Another water-bus was coming in out of the night with a full load of passengers, the thump of her diesel engines almost drowned by the music coming from her upper deck.

A launch was taking on people at a smaller jetty a few yards along, and Laird leaned against the walkway railing to watch. The launch had white paintwork, immaculate canvas awnings, and a shelter cabin with luxury seating. He became more interested as he saw her passengers. Some of the men going aboard had dinner jackets, the women wore mink and evening gowns.

As soon as the last passenger was aboard, the launch cast off with a low rumble of exhaust. Swinging round, heading out into the lake, she moved through the patch of light created by the water-bus piers.

Suddenly, without realising it, Laird gripped hard on the rough iron of the railing and stared at the name *Alton II* in bold, black lettering on the launch's stern.

The launch gathered speed and soon became lost in the dark expanse of the lake. Turning, Laird walked along to the jetty. It had a wooden gate with a small hut beside it, and a man emerged from the hut. He came over, a small, thin individual dressed like a sailor, with a peaked hat shoved far back on his head.

"Too late, *signore.*" He grinned and gestured across the lake. "But don't worry—she'll be back in half an hour."

"Back from where?" asked Laird.

"*Pero . . .*" The jetty attendant blinked. "Don't you want to go over to the Casino Rosa?"

"I might," said Laird amiably. "How's the action out there?"

"The best, *signore.*" The man relaxed again. "*Sì*, and no charge for the courtesy launch trip if you are on the list."

"I think I'd like to be on it, maybe tomorrow night." Laird reached into his pocket and folded some Swiss francs into the man's hand. "Could that happen?"

"*Grazie.* Any time, *signore.*" The money disappeared. "But bring your passport, okay? Over there is Italy. Jus' now and again some stupid *polizia* with nothing better to do can ask for such things."

"Passport." Laird nodded. "Who runs this Casino Rosa?"

The jetty attendant shrugged. "The owner is a Signor Stassen, a foreigner—people say he is from Belgium."

"Alton Stassen?"

"His first name is Paul." The man chuckled. "You saw the name on the boat, eh? He lives at the Villa Alton. The Casino Rosa is in the Villa grounds."

"Maybe I could have a look at the Villa too," said Laird. "Houses interest me."

"No, *signore*." The man's eyes widened at the idea. "The Villa is private property—very private. No one goes there."

"I never go where I'm not wanted," said Laird.

He said goodnight and left the man.

Further along the walkway a cluster of tourists, festooned with camera equipment and using tripods, were taking photographs of a floodlit series of water jets fanning up from a set of fountains located a little way out in the lake. The jets rose and fell, changed shape and colour with time-switch regularity, and brought cries of delight from the camera buffs. But Laird looked past them, out towards the dark line of land on the far side of the lake.

Alton was a house; the man behind it was called Paul Stassen. His mouth tightened as the water jets changed colour again and more cameras began a frantic clicking.

Lugano's lakeside was a playground. But so was another stretch of water, back in England, and they were linked by a cold, merciless act of murder.

He had still a long way to go.

It was close on midnight when he returned to the Hotel Orchidea. The streets outside were still busy; he'd walked through the town square, which seemed to amount to a whole series of pavement cafés offering music, beer, and beautiful girls, but the Orchidea took a more stolid view of things. The only light in the lobby was above the reception desk, where the same night clerk was sitting.

"*Allora*, Signore Laird." He was greeted with a beam of welcome. "Your cavalry trick—it worked like magic!"

"You won?" asked Laird. The chessboard was out of sight.

"I harassed him, chased him, tortured him with that knight." The night clerk slapped his plump hands together in delight. "Then, *sì*, the kill—all thanks to you." He leaned across his desk.

"People call me Jo-Jo. Any time you need anything, let me know. Okay?"

"I will," promised Laird, smiling. He paused. "Maybe you remember an Englishman who has been here a few times, a guest called Bullen Thoms?"

"A friend of yours?" asked Jo-Jo cautiously.

"No, just someone I met, back in London."

"I remember him." The man's face shaped a slight frown. "He would be hard to forget."

"Difficult?" suggested Laird sympathetically.

"*Sì*. Every time he complained about something."

"It sounds like him," said Laird. "Did he ever go across the lake to the Casino Rosa?"

The night clerk nodded. "He would come back late and boast about how much he had won. But even if they lose, they still say that, eh?"

"Did he have company?"

"Never. Not even a woman."

"Then it was really bad," said Laird solemnly.

He went up to his room, unlocked the door, and reached for the light switch.

"Good evening, Andrew Laird," said a voice from the darkness. A woman's voice, quiet, assured, and with a slight edge of amusement. "You've certainly kept me waiting."

A table lamp clicked on. The shaded pool of light shone on the dark-haired woman he'd seen at the reception desk when he'd been going out. She was sitting in one of the armchairs, a half-eaten pear in one hand, a faint smile on her lips.

"Come in and close the door," she suggested calmly. "And don't look so surprised—this is business."

"Who says?"

"My father." She settled deeper in the chair and crossed her trousered legs. "He probably didn't mention me. I'm Katie Holly, and my business is diamonds."

Laird swore to himself, went into the room, and closed the door.

CHAPTER FIVE

Too much had been happening, and Andrew Laird wasn't in a mood to accept anything or anyone at face value. Bleakly he considered the dark-haired woman still smiling up at him from the chair.

"Katie Holly. Can you prove it?"

She took another bite from the pear, then reached into the leather handbag at her feet and handed him a small plastic identity card. A diamond-shaped emblem, a built-in hologram image, seemed to quiver as Laird held it in the glow from the table lamp. The rest of the card held her photograph and signature above the printed words "Katherine Holly. Central Selling Organisation."

"Well?" She had been watching him. "Satisfied?"

"Central Selling—I've heard of them. Tell me about your father."

"He's on his way to New York—or there by now. He likes to pretend he's a dental mechanic, and I wish he'd get his hair cut more often." She grinned at him.

"I'm convinced." Laird made it an apology as Katie Holly took back the card and returned it to her bag. "But I've had a few problems."

"I've heard some of them."

They solemnly shook hands, and Laird sat on an edge of the bed, facing her. Katie Holly had a lightly tanned, outdoor complexion, the kind of smile which brought tiny laughter lines to life under her dark eyes, and white, regular teeth. Her only jewellery was a modest gold pendant with a small diamond set in its centre. He liked what he saw. She was a woman who was attractive rather than beautiful and who probably preferred it that way.

"I got hungry." She took another bite from the pear, then gestured apologetically towards the fruit basket on the table. "I helped myself."

"You're welcome." Laird smiled, trying to pin down the faint hint of an accent in her slightly husky voice. If anything, it was more American than British. "What was so important about waiting for me?"

"The sooner we talked, the better. I'm hoping we can help each other." Katie Holly eyed him seriously. "You're here to do a job; so am I. You don't want to trip over me; I don't want to trip over you."

"If that's how things are," said Laird. "But I'll give you a starting point. How did you get into this room?"

"I bribed a maid." She tossed what was left of the pear into a waste basket. "I told her I knew you were staying here, that we were old—uh—friends, and—"

"I'll guess the rest." Laird stopped her there. "Is your father behind any of this?"

She shook her head. "Not the way you mean. He didn't send me."

Laird sighed. "I don't know too much about the Central Selling Organisation. What am I buying?"

"All right, we're a marketing agency run by the diamond mining and trading associations, more or less world-wide. We're strictly commercial—even the Russians use us, though they don't shout about it." She chuckled softly. "The comrades have a big stake in the diamond world nowadays. They're major producers, with a lot of new mines. Maybe they don't compare with South Africa, but they're growing fast."

"So Central Selling is a kind of club?"

"Our job is to make sure the diamond market stays steady—"

"You keep the prices high?" suggested Laird.

"We keep them steady—at least we try." Katie Holly stayed patient. "That way, in the long run, everyone benefits. We control the flow of new stones reaching the market; we'll buy in and stockpile if demand falls, release extra parcels if there's a sudden shortage." She stopped and grimaced. "Look, Mr. Laird—"

"Andrew."

"Andrew. Do you really want the standard lecture at this time of night?"

"No," said Laird. "Just tell me about you, and exactly what the hell you're doing here."

"Thanks. All right, I'm with the C.S.O. Paris office, attached to what's called the Special Research Branch. If anything unusual happens, we find out why."

"Security?"

She hesitated, then nodded.

Laird frowned. "I thought diamond mining ran their own network."

"Against I.D.B.—theft and smuggling at mines, illicit buying from workers." She shook her head. "We're market-place, commercial, a lot more civilised and a lot less dangerous. Most of the time, anyway. The way this started—well, blame my father. Clanmore Alliance had him examine that batch of treated stones."

"In confidence," said Laird.

"On some pretty thin ethics," she countered. "My father is a gemmologist, with his own loyalties. That's why he contacted C.S.O. and told them about those stones." Her hands made a quick, explosive gesture. "That made a lot of people jump, and my boss was one of them."

"You make it sound like they were waiting on it," said Laird. He scraped a thumb along his chin. "Well?"

"Waiting for something," she corrected. "Look, Andrew, you've come here chasing a possible shipping fraud without really being sure it exists. What I'm chasing is just about as vague, someone spending more money than makes sense buying almost rubbish-quality diamonds."

Laird frowned his surprise. "Where?"

"Amsterdam—not always, but mostly."

"All being laser-treated?"

Katie Holly gave an amused half-sigh. "That's what we'd like to know. It looks that way—your London stones aren't the first to turn up. There haven't been many, but we know of two in New York, one in Munich, one in Rome, maybe two others in Tokyo. The Tokyo owner won't even talk about it."

"Feeling sick?"

"Sicker than sick."

"They all believed they were buying genuine, untreated stones?"

"All of them." She nodded. "One of the American diamonds was an investment purchase, at two hundred thousand dollars. An insurance valuer spotted it—a friend of my father. He reckoned it was actually worth thirty thousand; the insurance company refused cover."

"That happens," said Laird. "Old insurance man's proverb. When in doubt, run away from it." He could hear singing outside, several voices, growing louder against the background noise of the lakeside traffic. Getting up, he went over to the window and looked down. About a dozen young people were marching along under the streetlights, led by an umbrella-waving conductor. The song was Spanish; the words were being part sung, part shouted in German, French, and English. The marching, makeshift choir was enjoying itself—and a police car was tailing them at a discreet crawl. He chuckled and turned back to Katie Holly. "These stones—no way you can trace them back?"

"We've tried. We can't."

"And there could be more you don't know about?"

"There could be more even the owners don't know about," she said wearily. "Someone is making a killing; Central Selling wants him nailed."

"Before the diamond trade gets jittery?"

She nodded, rose, and came over to join him at the window. The marching singers, their voices beginning to fade, were already almost out of sight with the police car still trailing them. Beyond the busy, brightly lit lakeside, the night had become settled and clear. Far out in the lake, a water bus was heading north and leaving a narrow ribbon of wake which glinted white in the moonlight.

"Katie." Laird said her name quietly and waited until she faced him. He looked at her deliberately for a moment, something in her expression, in the way she suddenly seemed to go on guard, making him certain he was right. "What's the rest of it?"

"I—" She hesitated.

"Now," Laird suggested, "I want to hear it." He gave her a slight half-smile. "You won't scare me any more than has happened already."

"There's a story—it came to us from the Dutch police." She paused and fingered the little diamond pendant at her throat, her face grave. "They'd been told most of the money being used to buy these reject diamonds is coming from one of Amsterdam's biggest heroin dealers."

"How far did the police get with it?"

"There was a girl." She shrugged. "She was ready to talk—they found her body in a canal."

"It ended there?" asked Laird.

"Completely."

"Does the name Paul Stassen mean anything to you?"

"No." She shook her head.

The room seemed colder; the view across the lake had lost its attraction. But he should have expected it; there was always the same bottom-line situation—whenever something that mattered seemed ready to emerge, someone had died.

"Andrew." Katie Holly touched his arm. She was standing close to him, the musky scent of her perfume tantalising, but her face was serious. "Suppose you nail your shipping fraud? What happens?"

"We clear up the insurance backyard, warn a few friends, pass the rest to somebody's justice department—we're no private police force."

"We're the same. Our golden rule is 'find out—get out.' C.S.O. doesn't get involved, doesn't like publicity."

Laird nodded. Back in London, Osgood Morris would certainly have approved.

"How well do you know Lugano?"

"You're seeing my father's friend, Bernardo Garri." Katie Holly eyed him demurely. "As far back as I can remember, I've called him Uncle Bernardo."

He'd expected that. Resignedly Laird pointed towards the chair she'd left.

"Sit down," he invited. "You'd better hear why I want to talk with him. Or do you know already?"

"Only some of it," said Katie Holly. She settled in the chair, helped herself to the last apple in the basket, and took a firm, white-toothed bite. "I'll just eat."

A grey morning mist still clung in patches around Lake Lugano when Andrew Laird woke the next morning. It was close on eight A.M., traffic was already rumbling on the lakeside road, and he lay back for a moment listening to the muted noise.

It had been after midnight when Katie Holly had finally left.

They had talked, argued quietly once or twice. He'd told her most of the London story; she'd added a few details of the diamond-buying operation. Along the way, he'd picked up a few personal details about her: She was Miguel Holly's only child. Her mother had died while the girl was still in her teens. An American aunt had taken her almost forcibly across the Atlantic for schooling, but she'd been back with her father within a few years.

She knew her diamond trade. Holly had given her a start, apprenticing her to one of the biggest, toughest diamond-dealing firms in Europe. But after that, she'd made her own way.

Now he got out of bed and padded naked across to the window, frowning. They'd agreed to work together, yet separately. They each had some starting points; they each had their own problems.

He just hoped they got enough answers before trouble broke around them.

Showered and shaved, he phoned room service for a coffee-and-rolls breakfast. He was still dressing, tucking a blue shirt into dark corduroy trousers, buckling an old plaited leather seaman's belt at his waist, when a maid arrived with the tray. A raven-haired girl with a large bust and larger eyes, she put down the tray, then looked around.

"You slept well, *signore?*" she asked politely, glancing at the rumpled bed.

"Very well." Laird smiled his thanks, slipped his feet into a pair of rubber-soled moccasins, then realised she was still standing there. Sighing, he reached into his pocket for change.

"No, *grazie, signore*"—she giggled and looked at him in a way that didn't need interpreting—"the Signorina Holly took care of all that last night." She eyed the bed again and winked. "*Ecco* . . . we all hoped you liked your surprise, *signore.*"

Giggling again, she fled without waiting for an answer. Laird swore mildly as the door banged behind her, then grinned. He could think of worse fates than being linked with Katie Holly. Even if he hadn't earned the reputation he had apparently achieved with the Hotel Orchidea's staff, it might even be useful.

Still grinning, he used the telephone again and asked the hotel switchboard to call Katie Holly's room. There was no reply, and he hung up.

He ate breakfast at his window, watching the last of the morning mist being burned off by the sunlight, using one of the maps he'd brought, checking his geography against the emerging scenery.

What had seemed confusing by night was simple enough by day. Lake Lugano ran roughly north to south, a long, deep curve of water with Lugano itself flanking a bay on the west shore between two steep, wooded hills. The hill to the north was Monte Bre; the other, San Salvatore, had one face of almost sheer rock facing the lake, and he could see tiny cog-rail cars crawling up both of them.

Lips tightening, he switched his attention across the water, to the partly Italian shore. South of there, Milan was only about an hour's drive away. But the immediate view was of more harsh rock and wooded hills, then grey battalions of higher peaks and an occasional glint of white snow.

There were houses over there. Only a thin scattering, mostly close to the water, some in Italy, some Swiss—he shook his head. Geography and history couldn't have done better if they'd tried, producing two countries nuzzling so closely along a broken frontier of hills and passes. Add Lake Como to the east and Lake Maggiore to the west, add that main autoroute between Italy and Germany, and Lugano must be the answer to a smuggler's prayer.

He tried phoning Katie Holly's room again when he'd finished breakfast. There was still no reply, and he had a sneaking suspicion why. But it was also time he made a few moves of his own. He decided he wouldn't bother with a tie, pulled on a faded blue denim jacket he usually packed for trips, checked the pockets, then went down to the hotel lobby.

"Signore?" The day-shift clerk at the reception desk, a fair-haired young man in a red jacket, smelled strongly of cologne. "May I help you?"

"Can I send a telex from here?" asked Laird.

The clerk nodded and pushed a pad of telex forms across. Laird took a stub of pencil from his pocket, thought briefly, then wrote the few lines he needed. The telex was to Osgood Morris in London, the message apparently innocent but enough to start Morris's nose twitching:

"Zürich travel arrangements upset but Lugano as hoped so far.

Friendly competition here for collection you want. Bidding involves definite gamble. May look at lakeside property while here."

He took the telex form back and watched the desk clerk mutter his way through the words.

"I've to buy some old coins for a friend—he collects the things," lied Laird cheerfully. "They're going to cost more than he expected. Still, he can afford it. Better than I can."

"Anything old is expensive, Signor Laird," agreed the desk clerk sadly. He glanced at the telex message, then considered Laird again. "But if you are interested in property in Lugano, perhaps an apartment, I have a friend. Maybe if you talked to him—"

"*Grazie.*" Laird nodded vaguely. "Maybe later. Right now, I'm just looking."

He went outside. The air was warm, the pavements busy with people, and workmen with handcarts and brooms were clearing the last traces of debris left by the storm. Jewellery stores had restocked their window displays from their overnight strongrooms, the open-air cafés already had their first customers, women were queuing at a cake shop.

Katie Holly had given him directions. He followed the street signs along to the Piazza Riforma, then headed into the network of old, cobbled streets and narrow alleyways which lay behind it.

Bernardo Garri's shop, when he found it, was small and old-fashioned and half-hidden beneath an archway. It had bow-fronted windows, black paintwork, and offered the passer-by a jumbled display of silverware, medals, and old clocks. The name Garri was lettered on the door in faded gold paint, and a bell clanged as Laird pushed it open and entered.

Things weren't much different inside. The shop area was small, with bare wooden floorboards and a single neon-tube light. Battered glass-fronted cases were filled with medals, coins, and old banknotes. More of them were on a shelf behind the scarred wooden counter, along with a scattering of sad-looking pieces of second-hand jewellery.

A curtain at the back of the shop jerked open in a way that almost hauled it from its rail. A man in his fifties bustled out, overweight, bald, with a moon-like face which was already shaping a smile. He wore a grey wool cardigan over a white shirt, a stringy black tie, and dark trousers.

"Signor Laird?" Laird's hand was seized in a hairy, bear-like paw and pumped vigorously. "So, you come from Miguel Holly, eh? How is the old fool?"

"Fine. He sends his regards." Laird rescued his hand. "He hoped you could help me."

"He explained that, *al telefono.*" Garri chuckled. "You must tell me about him, later—that devil of a daughter of his says she hasn't seen him in months."

"She's been here?"

"For breakfast." Garri patted his ample stomach. "She had to leave. There are people she wants to see." A frown creased his broad face. "Damn the girl, for once I even agree with my wife. Why can't she marry, settle down, have babies? At her age—"

"Ask her," suggested Laird.

"Do I want both my legs broken?" Garri gave a mock grimace at the notion. Then he glanced past Laird. A man and a woman, dressed like tourists, both carrying airline flight bags, were peering at his window display. Sighing, Garri lifted the counter flap, reached the door with a surprising speed for his bulk, and snapped the lock closed just as the couple tried to come in. He shooed at them with his hands through the glass and gave a grunt of relief as they turned away. "I know that kind. Half an hour of your time, they try to bargain like Arabs; if they do buy, then they take the cheapest thing in the place—and they're back tomorrow wanting to change it. Come."

He led the way behind the counter, then through the curtain, and stopped, giving his visitor a sideways glance.

Laird stared. This side of the curtain had thick carpets, modern, softly lit display cases with glinting gold and silver coins, sparkling medals and enamelled badges. A selection of comfortable chairs were ranged round a low teak table. Towards the rear, a carpeted stairway led to an upper level.

"We live up there." Garri gestured overhead. "Here, this part, is for what you would call the carriage trade—but the front shop matters too. Between them"—he gestured a balancing see-saw with one hand—"I make a living. Are you interested in my kind of rubbish?"

Laird glanced around again. "I don't think I could afford it."

"The people I deal with back here collect as an investment, my friend," said Garri. "In the front shop I can sell you an Iron Cross or a Purple Heart, any kind of gold coin. I'll pay top price for one of your Falklands War medals. But back here we are different." Touching Laird's arm, he indicated the nearest display case, which held two small gold coins on a pad of purple velvet. "Gold ducats— Venice, thirteenth century. I'd like to keep them, but I can't afford them. Medals? Back here, I deal in Napoleon and Nelson."

Laird glanced along the display cases. "You're talking a lot of money."

"My bank manager says that each time I ask for a new loan." Bernardo Garri flopped down into one of the chairs in a way that made it squeak, and waved Laird into another. *"Mi scusi* . . . I'm wasting your time. It's the diamond painting—the magazine clipping I sent to Miguel Holly, eh?"

Laird nodded and stayed on the edge of his chair.

Garri shrugged. "There's no mystery. It was a charity art exhibition at our Museo Civico—the Villa Ciani. All the work of local artists. That one was exhibited by Signora Manton—Elsa Manton."

"So you know her?"

"Si." Garri stuffed his hands into the pockets of his cardigan, then sucked his lips appreciatively. "Austrian, good-looking, early forties maybe, and a widow—"

"A widow with money," said a dry voice behind them. "The fortunate kind. Painting isn't her only hobby."

Laird glanced round. The woman who had come quietly down the stairway at the back was small and neat, with dark hair going grey. She was dressed in a cream blouse and dark blue trousers, a single string of pearls at her throat.

"My wife, Anna." Garri grinned at her affectionately. "Treat her as an expert, Signor Laird—she hears most things."

"People interest me," she said. Laird had got to his feet, but she frowned and gestured him to sit again, then perched herself on the arm of her husband's chair. "Katie told me about you, Signor Laird. She said you were a Scot, not English. Is there much real difference?"

"A lot depends on who you ask." Laird smiled at her. "You know Elsa Manton?"

"I know about her," corrected Anna Garri. "She is Austrian. She was a dancer—ballet, not the other kind. Her husband died in a car accident. She was hurt but not badly—that was maybe four years ago, not long after they came here."

"From Lebanon," volunteered Garri. "Manton was Lebanese but half French"—he gave a sly wink at his wife—"and with that, there is a difference."

"Any idea why they left Lebanon?"

Garri shrugged and glanced at his wife. She shook her head.

"They had to sell some of her jewellery at first," said Garri slowly. "As if they were waiting for money coming."

Laird raised an eyebrow. "They came here?"

"No." The notion amused Garri. "To the big boys, the jewellers along the Via Nassa—then three months later, he was buying expensive pieces to replace them." He shrugged. "I heard about it after the crash."

"But only women gossip," said his wife innocently.

"Come back to the diamond painting," said Laird. "Where is it now?"

"Probably still with Elsa Manton," said Garri. "She had three canvases at the exhibition. It ran for a week; then everybody took their stuff home again."

"Is she any good?"

"As a painter?" Garri grinned, then yelped as his wife cuffed him lightly on the ear. "She'd never make a living at it."

"She hasn't that problem," said Anna Garri. Frowning, she straightened a crease on the front of her trousers. "The woman has her late husband's money; she can devote herself to being a grand lady of charity—and to other things." She looked up at Laird, a twist of a smile on her lips. "Other things like this man Paul Stassen, the one who interests you."

"Katie told us," explained Garri. He gave a quick, soothing gesture. "She thought it would save time."

"Go on," said Laird.

Garri shrugged. "I was asked if I knew anyone named Alton. I'm sorry—I wasn't too clever. I didn't think of the Villa Alton."

"But Stassen and Elsa Manton—"

"*Sì.*" Garri raised one hand, two fingers pressed close together, then nodded at his wife. "At least, Anna says that's the Lugano gossip."

"What about Stassen's background?"

Husband and wife exchanged a glance. Bernardo Garri hesitated.

"Nobody knows much," he admitted. "He has this Casino Rosa. He has other business interests. He seems to travel a lot. Give me a little time. There are people I could ask, friends." He paused, brightened, and started to lever his bulk out of the chair. "If it helps, I can show you where the Manton woman lives. It isn't far."

"I'll do that." Anna Garri pushed him down again and got to her feet. "He likes to forget he has work to do, Signor Laird. What about that American who is coming this morning?"

"*Sì,*" Garri said. "The one who collects medals. He wants that damn Serbian White Eagle."

"And he goes on to Rome tomorrow, where he might find something better," said Anna Garri. She held out her hand. "Car keys."

"Car keys." Garri gloomily fished in his pocket and dropped them into her palm. "If you're going spying, get some *benzina* on the way." He got up, ambled through to the front shop, and returned with a pair of binoculars in a battered leather case. "Take these. What about my lunch?"

"When I get back."

"*Sì.*" Garri looked at her soberly. "Anna, you just show him. No more."

"No more." She nodded, then smiled at Laird. "I'll get a jacket."

The shop had a back door. It led into a lane, and Laird followed the small, neat, very feminine figure of Anna Garri a short distance from there to the entrance of an underground *autosilo* garage. The Garris' car, a blue Fiat, was parked two floors down. She got behind the wheel, started the car as Laird settled in the passenger seat, then hit the accelerator. Tyres screaming, the Fiat snarled up the ramp to street level.

They kept to the back streets, climbing steadily until the lakeside was an occasional glimpse far below. On the outskirts of the town, the Fiat joined a winding, tree-lined avenue sprinkled with large, expensive homes, the kind with three-car garages, swimming pools, and well-manicured shrubbery.

"Almost there." Anna Garri dropped a gear to take the Fiat round another tight, climbing bend. "Signor Laird, how much do you really know about these people?"

"Only a little—enough to know they're dangerous." Laird braced himself as the Fiat swayed again. "Thinking of Katie?"

"*Sì.*" She gave him a quick, tight-lipped glance. "Katie says the *polizia* don't know of this yet."

Laird nodded. "Not in Lugano."

"If anything happens, they will—because I'll tell them." Anna Garri spoke with angry vehemence. "You understand, Signor Laird?"

As she spoke, she allowed the car to slow, then let it roll onto a narrow grass verge beside a thick, high hedge. Stopping on the handbrake, she switched off the engine, gave Laird the binoculars, and nodded towards his door.

They got out into the sunlight. The air was warm, birds were singing somewhere near, and after a small delivery van had driven past, heading downhill, the avenue was empty of traffic.

"About here should be right." Anna Garri beckoned him across to the hedge, found a gap in its leaves, peered through, then gave a pleased chuckle of surprise, stepped back, and pulled him nearer. "Quickly. You're in luck."

Pressing against the thorns of the hedge, Laird looked through the gap. It gave him a bird's eye view down across a steeply sloping garden to a modestly sized white villa with a red-tiled roof and the avenue's statutory swimming pool. The pool seemed drained, but that was incidental. He was looking almost directly at the villa's porch. A white Mercedes car waited on the gravel driveway, engine ticking over, exhaust murmuring gently, the driver's door lying open.

"That's her car," murmured Anna Garri, elbowing in again.

Laird took the binoculars, trained them on the porchway, and adjusted the focus. He lowered them quickly as a motor cycle stammered its way up the dusty avenue, then, once it had passed, used them again.

He was just in time. The woman coming out of the villa was tall and blond, her hair caught back by a clasp. She wore a cream linen skirt and jacket; she was probably in her early forties, and if she'd ever been a dancer, she'd put on weight since then.

"That's her," hissed Anna Garri. "And look—"

Laird nodded. Someone else was coming out from the porch. But he kept the lenses on Elsa Manton for a moment more. Her slightly angular face animated, a smile on her lips, she turned to talk to the man behind her. Laird followed with the binoculars, then froze.

It was the thin, dark-haired man he'd seen at Zürich Airport, the man who had met the fat, cutlery-stealing David Trimble from London. Trimble, who had been carrying Laird's photograph and who had died under the rail-link locomotive. He listened to the blond woman, nodding attentively, smiling dutifully. The dark-suit image of Zürich had gone; he was in a sports shirt, tan corduroy trousers, and suede boots.

"Is that Stassen?" he asked tensely.

Anna Garri shook her head. "No. Paul Stassen has red hair and is broader. I don't know that one."

Elsa Manton and her escort got into the Mercedes, the blond woman taking the driving seat, the dark-haired man hovering to close the door for her, then getting in on the passenger side.

"How about following them?" asked Laird quickly.

"I can try." Anna Garri was doubtful but nodded. "They'll go down towards the town. The other way, up the hill, comes to a dead end."

The Mercedes was moving. They hurried back aboard the Fiat, turned, and started down the hill. They saw the Mercedes ahead, already out of the driveway and purring down towards the town.

Elsa Manton was apparently in no hurry; following her wasn't difficult. But she wasn't heading in towards Lugano. Halfway down the hill she turned right at a main-road junction and settled into the traffic flow. The Fiat followed, Anna Garri gradually becoming more confident, letting the gap between the two cars widen with other vehicles between them.

"Where are we heading?" asked Laird.

"The frontier—it's only a few kilometres. Or it might—yes, it might be before there, the airstrip at Agno." Anna Garri sounded worried. She pointed to the fuel gauge. "Bernardo was right. We need *benzina.*"

The fuel-gauge needle was almost at empty. The small, dark-haired woman began making soft, coaxing noises under her breath, then gave a sigh of relief. The white Mercedes was slowing; its turn indicators were flashing.

"It's the airstrip," she said thankfully.

Two minutes later they had stopped in the shelter of some huts on the edge of Agno airstrip. The white Mercedes had disappeared somewhere ahead, among the larger buildings.

"This is as far as you go," said Laird gratefully. "Get some *benzina.* Get yourself back home. You've done enough."

She blinked in surprise. "What about you?"

"I'll have a look around; then I'll make my own way back." Laird saw the protest starting to shape. Quickly, gently, he brought her chin round and kissed her lightly on the lips. *"Grazie,* Anna . . . Bernardo is a lucky man."

"I was starting to enjoy myself." She sighed and gave in.

Laird left the Fiat, waited while it turned and bumped back towards the road, then walked on. He could hear a plane somewhere overhead. It sounded small and piston-engined, and if it was coming in to land, Laird didn't envy the pilot.

Level ground had to be at a premium in the area. The Agno airstrip, a single-tarmac runway, seemed alarmingly short and ran roughly north to south down a narrow valley. There were rising, scrub-covered hills to either side; the approach from the north looked as though it involved scraping in over cloud-capped peaks, and the south approach, in over an arm of Lake Lugano, meant weaving between more high ground and rock.

It wasn't his problem, but that incoming flight might be. Laird moved on, walking boldly along the perimeter road, making no attempt to avoid being seen. Half a dozen light aircraft were parked on the grass verges, outside a hangar building. Agno had offices and a windsock, a radio mast, and a couple of small servicing tenders. A mechanic was working on one of the aircraft, and music was coming from one of the huts. Then he saw the white Mercedes again, parked outside of what seemed to be a clubhouse.

Elsa Manton was standing beside it, looking to the north. The aircraft he'd heard was coming in, a tiny, twin-engined shape, dipping and losing height, wheels lowering.

The nearest cover was an old biplane, lying empty and deserted on a patch of hard standing. Laird reached it, still felt exposed, and on an impulse swung himself up into the cockpit and stayed there.

The incoming aircraft, a Cessna, touched down lightly. Engines throttled back; it taxied on along the tarmac, then swung in towards the white Mercedes. The twin arcs of the propellors slowed and chunked to a halt, the cabin door swung open, and two men climbed down to talk briefly, then separate.

One, wearing a leather jacket and carrying a set of head-phones, was obviously the pilot. He went towards the clubhouse building, giving a cheerful wave in Elsa Manton's direction. The other man headed straight towards her. Medium height, stockily built, with coppery red hair, he wore a smartly cut grey business suit and carried a black briefcase. When he reached Elsa Manton, she gave him a quick, welcoming hug.

Staying low in the biplane's open cockpit, Laird watched. The new arrival had to be Paul Stassen; he matched the description Anna Garri had given him—and as the couple turned toward the Mercedes, the dark-haired man emerged from it like a Jack-in-the-box. Stassen tossed him the briefcase, and nodded at something the man said; then Stassen and the woman got into the back of the car, and their companion took over as chauffeur.

The Mercedes started and purred past Laird's biplane shelter. He had a brief, close glimpse of Stassen through the car's lightly tinted windows as it went by in a scatter of gravel, heading for the main road. The man from the Villa Alton, the man he'd come to Switzerland to locate, had a strong, almost ugly face, long hair, and was also probably in his mid-forties. He lounged back in the rear seat, lighting a cigarette, Elsa Manton close beside him.

The car reached the road, turned left in the direction of Lugano, and vanished from sight. Laird levered himself out of the biplane's tight-fitting cockpit, climbed down, and heard a shout as his feet touched the ground. The mechanic who had been working at the hangar was coming towards him, a large spanner in one hand.

"Finito," shouted Laird and waved cheerfully. "Everything's fine."

The mechanic hesitated, puzzled. Laird waved again and began walking unhurriedly towards the road. He glanced back, and the mechanic had stopped.

"*Grazie* . . ." Laird grinned and nodded, and the mechanic shrugged and turned away.

He caught a bus back into Lugano, rode as far as the lakeside, then walked the short distance to the Hotel Orchidea. Some departing guests were getting aboard a mini-bus, and the same young desk clerk with the red jacket and the overkill cologne was making agitated noises around a couple of porters loading luggage.

For the moment nothing else obviously mattered or existed. Laird stopped at the reception desk, saw two envelopes in the pigeonhole rack at his room number, went round behind the desk, and helped himself.

"Signor Laird!" An outraged cry came from the clerk. "No, that is not allowed. That is my job—"

"And no one does it better," soothed Laird.

Coming out, leaning on the desk, he opened the envelopes. One was a telephone message slip. Osgood Morris had telephoned from London and wanted Laird to call back immediately. Laird opened the other envelope and unfolded a brief scribble on hotel notepaper. It was from Katie Holly. It said simply, "Water-bus terminal, noon. I'll buy lunch."

The lobby clock showed he had only a few minutes left to get there. Osgood Morris would have to wait. Crumpling both notes, tossing them into a waste basket, he elbowed his way out again past the continuing battle over the mini-bus luggage.

Noon was a rush-hour time in Lugano. Laird loped along the crowded pavements, then cursed as he reached the lakeside road directly opposite the water-bus piers. The road was a noisy, horn-blasting, nose-to-tail rush of traffic in both directions with a pent-up crowd of pedestrians already trapped at the kerb. An old woman at the front shook an angry umbrella, then screamed and swore as a boy on a motor cycle grabbed it from her and kept on going.

He could see Katie Holly in a floppy powder-blue sweater and white trousers, standing at the entrance to one of the piers where a large white boat was loading. He waved, but she didn't see him.

Suddenly someone cheered. Pushing forward, a buxom young policewoman marched straight out into the road. She wore a white blouse, red skirt, and peaked hat; she stood solid as a rock in flat black shoes and heavy brown tights, raised a hand, and the traffic shuddered to a reluctant halt.

The torrent of pedestrians flowed across, Laird among them. As he passed, he saw that she had opened her shoulderbag with her free hand and was taking out a lipstick.

He'd have given her any of Bernardo Garri's medals as he hurried the last few yards to where Katie Holly was standing.

"You made it!" The frown on her face vanished as he arrived and she grabbed his arm. "Come on, I've got the tickets."

He had no chance to argue. She hustled him along the creaking wooden pier, pushed the tickets into the hand of a uniformed crewman, and they tumbled aboard the water-bus. A bell clanged, a klaxon gave a short blast, and the gangway was hauled in behind them.

"Where are we going?" asked Laird, bewildered. "You said lunch—"

"And I'm still paying." She grinned at him, while a stray breeze from the lake towsled her dark hair. "I can't get you any ocean waves, but how about a drink and a sandwich afloat?"

"Why not?" The water-bus was shuddering, already beginning to throb out into the lake. Laird looked at her again, sensing something more. "You've a reason?"

She nodded, grabbing a rail as the boat gave another shudder and gathered speed.

"You'll get a close-up view of the Villa Alton and the Casino Rosa on this trip—budget price." She paused. "You're still interested?"

"More than ever." Laird matched her grin. "Can we eat first?"

"My department." She left him, going down a companionway stair to queue at the little cafeteria bar on the lower deck.

Laird leaned on the rail. The water-bus, a shallow-draught craft about sixty feet long, was already well out from the shore, and the water beneath her had that impenetrable blackness which meant a lot of depth. He glanced back at the white wake churning from her stern, then switched a professional interest to the tiny bridge area just above him.

Like any dry-land bus, she showed a destination board. The skipper-helmsman at the controls had a seat, a truck-type steering wheel, gear-change, and instrument layout. From the sound of the engines, motive power came from a couple of diesels. Laird caught himself wondering how the high-decked craft handled in the kind of storms that must sweep down from those mountains. Probably she ran for cover.

He would. The water-bus men, with their land-locked little ships, faced their own kinds of danger.

He let the thought end there as Katie Holly returned triumphant, hugging a massive white bread and cheese sandwich for each of them along with two tiny plastic packs of white wine to be drunk through a straw.

They found an empty seat with a small table near the stern. Feeding the straw into her wine pack, Katie Holly took a long swallow and made a contented noise.

"I haven't had too good a day," she admitted. "It's been win some, lose some."

"Then we're level." Laird watched as she used both hands on the monster sandwich and took a first bite from it. The breeze ruffled her hair again, over her eyes, and she used a sleeve to brush it back. For the moment, it wasn't easy to relate the way she was to the cool, poised woman of the previous evening. "What did you get?"

She shook her head, still chewing. "You first. I looked in on Anna and Bernardo; she said she'd dropped you at the airport. What happened?"

"Paul Stassen flew in."

"And?" She seemed to sense there was more.

Laird told her about the dark-haired man with Elsa Manton, and she pursed her lips for a moment, suddenly serious again, frowning.

"I wonder—" She said it softly, the words almost lost under the throb of the diesels and the sound of churning water.

"Do I get to hear?" asked Laird.

"I've got a tie-in on the diamonds side, pretty positive." One of the lakeside birds swooped in close to them, banked away, then came back again. Absently she tore off a corner of bread from the sandwich and threw it over the side. The bird snatched the bread before it reached the water, then soared off. "I checked round the main jewellery people in town, people Bernardo reckoned I could trust—and he should know. I asked if they'd had any offers of loose diamonds."

"And?"

"I was asking the wrong questions; I was just lucky I got the right answers." She scowled as the bird tried swooping again. "Look at that thing—it's a vulture in disguise."

"Katie." Laird said it patiently. "What did you get?"

"Two Lugano jewellery firms, almost the only two who do any manufacturing on the premises, have had the same man as a customer within the last month. He bought what they call trade supplies—first time round, it was a special diamond-cutting paste from one of them. Then he came back trying to get a replacement drive belt for a bruting machine." She saw Laird was puzzled. "It's a sort of lathe for finishing after cutting. They remember he knew what he was talking about."

The water-bus klaxon gave a sudden hoot; the engines altered their rhythm. They were swinging in towards the shore again, making for a lakeside village which had its own small pier.

"This man"—Laird knew Katie Holly had her own priorities—"did he give them any kind of story?"

"Vague noises about being an amateur gemmologist and that he'd come to live in the Ticino." She saw the next question coming and shook her head. "No, he was grey-haired, late fifties or early sixties, fairly small. He said his name was Schmidt."

Laird shrugged his disappointment, and she gave a chuckle.

"Wait. The staff at both firms remember two things about him. First he had a small diamond set into his left thumbnail. Real workshop pros in the trade sometimes do that." Her face softened. "My father did, when he was younger. They drill a hole in the nail, then have to renew it every now and again as the nail grows." She paused deliberately, tantalisingly. "But here's what you maybe want, Andrew. This 'Schmidt' was never alone. He always had a younger, dark-haired man with him—hanging around like a cross between a watchdog and a minder. If he bought anything, the younger man paid."

Laird moistened his lips. Dark-haired men came two a penny. But he was ready to gamble on this one; he had to be another link in the growing, firming chain.

Diamonds and a shipping fraud, or a shipping fraud and diamonds—either way, whatever the emphasis, he thought of the rest, from murder onward. It was taking on the size and shape of a butcher's bill, but if drug peddling was the third somehow related element, then anything had to be expected.

"We're both in business, Katie," he said softly.

She nodded, her mouth a tight, thoughtful line. "So what do we do about it?"

"Right now?" They were easing in towards the pier. There was a bustle of activity on the tiny bridge; two crewmen were fussing at the gangway. Laird gave her a crooked grin. "We take the cruise, see the sights—do some thinking."

The sun was warm; the surface of the lake did little more than ripple in the breeze. He took a sip of wine, then a first bite at his sandwich. The cheese was strong and smokey-flavoured, the bread freshly baked. He took another casual glance at the pier; then his eyes strayed back to Katie Holly.

"Something wrong?" she asked.

Laird shook his head.

But she'd caught him fantasising. She'd been part of it; he was glad she couldn't read minds.

The water-bus bumped the pier, and Andrew Laird reached again for his carton of wine. If he had to plan a small war, there were worse ways of doing it.

CHAPTER SIX

The water-bus had a mixed load of passengers, a few disembarking at each small pier, a few more coming aboard. She was carrying a number of round-trip tourists, but the majority of people were locals —women on their way home after a day's shopping in town, a young soldier with his leg in plaster, two middle-aged officials with brief-cases.

Laird watched the determined bustle at each stop with an amused respect. Water-bus timetables were obviously sacred; any latecomer galloping towards a pier was something to be ignored and left be-hind.

As the white boat thudded out from another stopping place, a prosperous lakeside suburb of speedboats and swimming pools, he frowned again at the indicator board below the bridge. Capiso, the village pier for both the Casino Rosa and the Villa Alton, was the halfway point on the round-trip cruise. The indicator board showed a twenty-minute scheduled stop, a tiny green, white, and red Italian flag painted beside it.

"Got your passport?" asked Katie Holly.

He nodded and patted his jacket pocket.

"Good." She opened her handbag and showed him the cover of her own. "Usually they just count heads, coming and going—and that's if they're feeling energetic. But—"

"But let's not make waves." Laird nodded. "I'm not complaining. Anything I should know about what's over there?"

"Not really." She leaned her elbows on the deckrail. "I told you, it's a little outcrop of Italy. There's another, older casino lower down the lake, at Campione, but that's if you want bright lights and music —if you want action, the word is go for the Casino Rosa."

They came in for another stop, an old village built into a cliff and tied up under carved wooden balconies close to a garbage chute.

Someone's newly washed patchwork quilt hung drying on a pulley-rope, and the houses nearest the water's edge had brick-arched boat-houses instead of basements.

From there they sailed close in under the shadow of a steep mountain of rock, a shadow where the air temperature plunged. A jaunty blast on the white boat's klaxon vibrated and echoed off the rock; then the skipper-helmsman at the controls swung his wheel, and they headed across the width of the lake towards the opposite shore.

They came back into the sunshine. A sailing boat crossed their bows; then the eastern shore, a high ridge of hills thinly scattered with houses, welcomed them. Their first stop, a tiny village with a church, had Italian and Swiss flags flying side by side on the pier, and a Swiss customs man had a shouted conversation with two of the crew.

Capiso was to the south. To get there meant sailing close to a long, high line of black rock. Here and there the deep water swirled in strange eddying patterns of trapped leaves and larger debris. Even in the sunlight, even with a background of music coming from a radio on the lower deck, it was a stretch which looked both un-friendly and inhospitable.

"Andrew." Katie Holly nudged Laird. "Up there."

A large villa was perched on the edge of the rock above them. It had walls of pale cream stone, a steep roof of red clay tiles, and a central turret. He had a glimpse of a high boundary fence; then, as the boat travelled on, a bank of shrubbery hid everything from sight.

"Ever been there?" he asked.

"Just once, when I was a child." She shook her head. "All I remember is it used to be owned by an old woman, a widow."

They passed a private landing stage with a path leading up to-wards the villa. A small, fast launch was tied to the landing stage and had the name *Alton I.* Then the water-bus made a final, tight turn round a headland and into a small bay. The Italian flag flew at a pier, and Laird saw the big passenger launch *Alton II,* the one he'd seen loading passengers for the casino the previous night, berthed alongside. A handful of small houses were scattered beside the pier, and a large two-storey building with panoramic glass windows sat to one side. It was topped by a man-sized concrete rose, and a neon sign spelled out *Casino Rosa*.

The water-bus tied up at the pier, her loudspeakers announced the twenty-minute stop, and her passengers began to pour ashore.

Laird and Katie Holly went with them. There was a customs hut, but it was empty. An Italian customs officer, in khaki uniform, lounged in a chair in a patch of shade beside a boathouse. He nodded casually in their direction.

"That's it?" asked Laird.

Katie nodded, saw the customs officer glance at them again, smiled in the man's direction, and took Laird's arm.

"Unless there's trouble or someone important comes calling." She gave a slight shrug. "It's that kind of frontier, Andrew—always has been. Half the people who work in Lugano have their homes in Italy and commute daily. It's the same for shopping, business, and a lot more."

"What about smuggling, illegal immigration?"

"What about it? Ask the Garris—or Jo-Jo at the hotel." She chuckled and raised her free hand, the fingers tightly together. "The authorities on both sides, Italian and Swiss, work like that. If it matters, one of them usually knows—if one knows, both know."

The tourist swarm began spreading out, investigating a couple of small bars and a souvenir shop which had once been a fisherman's cottage. Laird guided Katie beyond them, gradually working nearer to the casino building.

Close up it was larger than he had realised. Staff were setting tables at a ground-floor bar and restaurant. He caught a glimpse of a broad terrazzo stairway leading up to the gaming rooms, and they passed a gardener using a rake and broom around the flower beds which flanked the casino entrance. Someone had spent a lot of money trying to get things impressively right.

But the scene was different behind the casino, where the ground began rising. The same high fence guarding the Villa Alton from the lake was continued, concrete posts carrying netting and topped by a vicious triple weave of barbed wire. A single road from the pier was guarded by padlocked metal gates topped by more barbed wire.

Visitors might be welcome at the Casino Rosa, but the way from there was tightly controlled.

They strolled on. No one challenged them, and they reached the fence. On the far side the steep slope was a green carpet of scrub and coarse grass, but there wasn't so much as a glimpse of a chimney to show that Villa Alton existed. Laird considered the fence. It was good enough to serve its purpose. Anyone wanting to get through would need heavy-duty wire-cutters and a lot of time.

"Keep out, stay out," murmured Katie Holly. "Not very friendly. What about that landing stage—the one with the fast launch?"

"It'll be the same—probably worse," said Laird grimly.

She shrugged, looking back the way they had come. The gardener had stopped working; the mound of leaves and rubbish he'd gathered had vanished. He was sitting on an upturned bucket, lighting a cigarette, and what had to be the lid of a metal manhole cover was propped beside him.

"My father has his own approach to a problem. If you want to know something, ask. Do me a favour, Andrew—admire the view or just get lost. I'm going to ask about gardening."

She left him, walking in a deliberate, hip-swinging way. Laird saw her reach the gardener and watched the grin spread on the man's leathery, unshaven face as she spoke. The cigarette vanished from his mouth, he got to his feet, and in another moment he was talking animatedly while they stood examining the nearest display of flowers. Behind her back, Katie flicked a hand to Laird in a "go away" gesture.

He left her to it and went over to the pierside souvenir shop. When she joined him there, he was trying to appear interested in a display of souvenir dolls.

"You look more the teddy bear type." She glanced along the dolls. "Still, how about that little blonde at the end?"

"How about your garden gnome?"

"My helpful garden gnome," she said smugly. "There's an easy way to avoid that fence. You go under it—at worst you might get your feet wet."

One of the shop staff, a girl in Swiss costume, came towards them.

"*Prego, signorina*— " Her eyes strayed to Laird, and she smiled. "Can I help you?"

"*Sí.*" Katie pointed at a small, cheap brooch of a mountain goat, set with coloured glass eyes. "Him. He reminds me of someone."

Laird paid for the brooch and waited while she pinned it on the front of her sweater.

"So how about your garden gnome?" he asked again.

"There's a small stream—one they couldn't divert when they built the casino. It runs through a culvert from beyond the fence and comes out beside the pier."

Laird shaped a soft whistle. "What size of culvert?"

"Big enough to cope with flash floods from the hills, he says. But most of the time it is almost dry."

They walked to the pier, stopped where the *Alton II* was tied up, and pretended to admire the casino launch. Laird touched Katie's arm, and she gave a fractional nod. The culvert exit, a round, brick-faced hole, was at the bottom of a low stone wall. The gardener hadn't lied; only a thin trickle of water was dribbling out towards the lake—and if the culvert stayed that size all its distance, a man could walk through at a slight crouch.

"There could be something nasty, like a grille at the other end," said Katie. "I didn't ask—I'm sorry."

Laird shrugged. The stone wall ran along the lakeside for a short distance, then joined a flight of steps. He tried to picture how it would be by night, with the casino lights and patches of shadow.

It could be done; it was worth the risk.

A warning hoot came from the water-bus. Her diesels had started up again; passengers were returning aboard.

"Seen enough?" asked Katie.

"For now." Laird rubbed one foot along the ground and frowned at the mark he'd made. "Got anything arranged for tonight?"

"No." She considered him warily.

"We could come back tonight, take a turn around the gambling tables—"

"You mean you want to try for the Villa?"

Laird nodded. "It shouldn't be too hard. We come in the front door as far as the casino is concerned. But I try for the house on my own—one of us has to stay on the outside, in case things go wrong."

"Damn you." Her eyes showed she knew he was right. Glancing

again at the culvert, she sighed. "I suppose there are rats in there anyway."

"Probably hungry ones."

She gave a reluctant grin. "Suppose your dark-haired friend from Zürich turns up at the tables?"

Laird shrugged. That was a different kind of gamble.

A longer warning blast from the water-bus saved him from more of an answer. They followed the other passengers trooping aboard, then found a place at the rails as the little ferry shuddered her way out from the pier.

They cleared the bay as another boat, an open launch with faded paintwork and a noisy engine, came in trailing a dirty blue cloud of stinking exhaust smoke. The two craft passed at about a stone's throw distance apart, but the group of men seated in the launch's open cockpit showed no interest.

The cloud of exhaust smoke reached the water-bus. One of her crew yelled an insult at the launch, then followed it with a high-speed outburst in Italian to one of his companions. The second man laughed and turned away.

"What was that about?" asked Laird.

Katie grinned. "Without the adjectives? Everyone on that launch has an unusual line in parents; they all deserve drowning except it would foul the lake, and I'll miss the rest." Her mouth tightened a little. "Except for who they are—that's the night-shift squad of hired heavies at the casino."

The stink of exhaust smoke was still in the air. The launch-load of guards vanished from sight, turning in towards the pier. Almost everything probably came in by boat from the Swiss side. From Italy things were obviously different. Anything coming up from the Milan direction could use the main autoroute.

Anything. Laird looked out at the smooth surface of the lake, hardly seeing it, fighting a sense of frustration. He needed some kind of a breakthrough; it had to come. But—

"Have you totally stopped listening to people?" asked Katie with irritated sarcasm.

"Sorry." He gave a grin. "I was switched off."

"I noticed. All right, I'll try again. Does Clanmore Alliance insure things like this boat, or do you only handle ocean-going size?"

"If it floats, if the premium rate is right, we'll take anything," said Laird truthfully. "Even if we don't like a risk, we won't turn it down —we just jack up the premium so high the owner goes away."

"Business ethics." She said it dryly. "You told me about the coffee cargo fraud. This—could it be something similar?"

"It could. But someone always keeps coming up with a new angle."

Or it seemed that way. Ships could be sunk, ships could disappear. Sometimes the ones that disappeared turned up later with a new name, a new paint job, a new crew but the same owner, in a different part of the world.

Cargo cover could be another maze. Claims might be filed for late deliveries because a market had been missed. But sometimes a cargo would be shipped that no one really wanted to arrive. He could have told her about the load of frozen meat, condemned on arrival in Europe because a ship's refrigeration plant had broken down during the voyage. Clanmore had paid out because there was no option. The seller had thrown a party; the European buyer had bought a new yacht; the ship's chief engineer had acquired a new car.

There were plenty more. He wondered what the slim, poised woman beside him would have thought of the man who made a living out of shipping broken-down racehorses from Britain to Australia. The horses were always over-insured; the groom travelling with them had orders to make sure they took sick and died during the voyage. Ships weren't equipped to handle dead racehorses—the carcass was dumped in mid-ocean. There was nothing the insurance companies concerned could do but pay out—until at last they'd caught on to what was happening.

"Will it do if I shut up, or should I take a walk around the deck?" asked Katie Holly pointedly.

"Sorry." He touched her arm and gave an apologetic grimace. But a thought had stirred in his mind. They'd broken the racehorse racket by planting a young insurance clerk into a training stable as an apprentice. He wondered. "Ever thought of taking flying lessons?"

"Me?"

"You."

"With or without wings?"

"With." Laird grinned at her. "At the Agno airstrip. Tell them you're holidaying, with money to spend. Chat them up."

"About flying—then about Paul Stassen?"

He nodded.

"Why not?" She liked the idea. "But I want to talk to Bernardo and Anna again, and I'll have to call Paris. My man with the diamond thumbnail will mean something to them."

"How about asking Bernardo?"

"I will. But diamond craftsmen at that level have their own tight little world, and Bernardo isn't part of it." She shivered a little. A strong, gusting breeze had come out of nowhere and was ruffling the lake. Some passengers were already heading for shelter below deck. "Where will you be?"

"Checking some London leads. If I don't do it, they'll want to know why."

"My car is at the water-bus terminal." She produced the keys from her handbag and gave them to him. "You use it—I'll borrow Anna's Fiat." She stopped his half-formed thanks. "You can buy dinner."

There were another half-dozen stops on the way back to Lugano, most of them small villages. But at last the ferry boat came in towards the busy terminal, berthed, and began unloading. The terminal area was already crowded with people, some waiting on friends, others queuing to join boats, but Laird heard their names shouted as he followed Katie ashore. Bernardo Garri elbowed his way towards them, a smile on his broad moon-like face, and gave Katie a cheerful hug.

"Enjoy your trip, Signor Laird?" he asked good-humouredly, then turned to Katie. "*Bella* . . . you have some colour in your cheeks, the way a woman your age should have."

"All right, Bernardo—I know the rest of the lecture." She scowled affectionately at him. "Where's Anna?"

"At the shop, waiting for us."

"Heard anything more?" asked Laird.

"Nothing that matters." Bernardo Garri said it ruefully and ran a hand over his bald head. "Still, we'll keep trying. But—ah—let's not keep Anna waiting too long, eh? She has some things of her own to do this afternoon."

"I'm ready now," said Katie.

She winked at Laird and left with the big shopkeeper.

Another water-bus was coming in, more people were pushing forward, and Laird had to shoulder his way through as he headed for the other exit, closer to where Katie had left her car. But as he reached the edge of the crowd, he spotted a familiar face, changed direction, and caught up with the fat figure of Jo-Jo, the Hotel Orchidea's night clerk.

"Signor Laird!" The man's heavy face creased in a forced, startled smile. "Enjoying your stay?"

"Finding my way around, Jo-Jo." Laird gave him another glance. The night clerk was out of uniform, dressed in a grey, long-sleeved sweatshirt and a pair of faded denim trousers which were too tight across the seat. "What brought you here?"

"I was to meet someone—a friend, Signor Laird." The night clerk shrugged awkwardly, gave a quick, anxious look around, then brightened. "I think maybe—si, I think I see him now."

He plunged away and vanished.

Frowning, Laird watched him go, then set off again. He found the green Opel coupe, a parking ticket under one of the wiper blades, pocketed the ticket, and got aboard. There was a street map in the glove compartment. He studied it, then started the car and began driving.

Lugano's main post office was located, sensibly enough, on the Via della Posta. Laird left the car nearby, skirted a patch of open square where a bearded young pavement artist was working with chalk on an Alpine scene featuring life-size cattle, and went into the building. He had to change some paper money for a handful of Swiss franc coins; then he located a vacant public phone booth. Inside the door closed; he fed money into the coin slot as he dialled Clanmore Alliance's international trunks number.

Osgood Morris was in a meeting when he got through to London. But within moments the marine claims manager came on the line in almost breathless fashion.

"Where the hell have you been?" his high-pitched voice squeaked indignantly. "You send a damned fool telex message I'm supposed to understand. You—" He stopped suddenly. "Is this line secure?"

"Better than my hotel," said Laird laconically. "Not a bug in sight. How's Jerry Reilly?"

"Improving. Recovered enough to have begun annoying his nurses," said Morris impatiently. "I'm more interested in you. I know about the Zürich thing—at least, I know some salesman who was on your flight ended up under a train. How much of a connection?"

"He was carrying my photograph. I don't think he wanted it autographed."

Morris gave a groan. "So they have you—"

"In the picture," agreed Laird and regretted it. Osgood Morris hadn't that kind of sense of humour.

"What about this 'lakeside property'?"

"Alton isn't a man's name. It's a place." Laird sketched the situation. He had to feed the slot more coins before he finished. "Paul Stassen—does he mean anything, Osgood?"

"No. But this Manton woman—I've heard her name. Charity work, something like that—" Morris's natural caution took over. "Well-connected?"

"Maybe. How much does it matter?"

"Nothing to me, but the chairman may ask. Drugs, diamonds, gambling, another damned death—I don't like any of it. He broke off long enough to snap at someone trying to talk to him at his end of the line, then started again. "There's nothing fresh here—or at Poole. I've been in touch with Bullen Thoms's wife. She's arranging to fly home; she obviously knows nothing—probably cares about as little. But you—ah—mentioned 'friendly competition,' Andrew. Explain."

"Holly's daughter. She's here; she's with a diamonds outfit called Central Selling Organisation."

"I see. Yes, of course—friendly competition." The marine claims manager sounded oddly relieved. "You—so that was really all you meant, nothing else?"

"Yes." A suspicion flared in Laird's mind, then took a moment longer to form.

"I know C.S.O.—by reputation, anyway." Morris made it a purr. "Is she helping?"

"Maybe more than you are."

"More?" Morris made a surprised noise.

"Give me a straight answer, Osgood," said Laird softly. "I've seen another man killed; I've stuck my neck out further than I like. What else is going on out here?"

"I don't understand you." Morris sounded stiff, nervous, almost agitated.

"I think you do, Osgood." Laird shifted his position in the little telephone booth and looked out at the people going past. It was the same vague feeling he'd had a couple of times back in London, but stronger, still growing. He was used to operating on his own, but something wasn't right; it was as if he was being used, manipulated. "Is anyone else working on this?"

For a long moment Morris didn't answer. Then a resigned sigh came over the line.

"Yes."

"Who?"

"I can't tell you. I—I'm not totally sure." The marine claims manager stumbled over the words. "Other people are interested in —well, in what we're doing. You understand?"

"No," said Laird.

"They're friendly; they're not competition." Morris's voice came tightly. "Anything I'm doing is on our chairman's direct instructions. You—you get paid to do a job. Get on with it."

The line went dead. Morris had hung up.

Swearing under his breath, Laird slammed his own receiver down and walked angrily out of the booth. He collided with a woman, apologised quickly, and slowed down. Outside he stopped where the pavement artist was still busy with his chalks. The Alpine scene was shaping, going more commercial, taking in the figure of a busty milkmaid. He watched the man work, his anger gradually abating. Morris had said get on with it; there wasn't much else he could do.

He tossed some coins into the pavement artist's hat and went on, to where he'd left the Opel. It was time he checked out the London list covering Bullen Thoms's credit card transactions around Lugano.

Bullen Thoms had eaten at the best restaurants, had visited only the best shops. For the next couple of hours Laird found himself criss-crossing Lugano as he went systematically down the list.

At some stops a glance from the outside was enough. At others he went in and talked to the staff. Only twice—at a restaurant, then at a liquor store—did anyone remember the English shipbroker, each time because of a display of brutish ill-temper.

But it was outside the liquor store that Laird first suspected he was being tailed. The car was a small yellow Lancia, an old model, and it had pulled in about half a block behind his when he parked the Opel. Somehow he knew he had seen it before. When he returned to the Opel, the Lancia was still there. It was grubby and dusty; there seemed to be only the driver aboard.

Laird watched his rear view mirror as he set the Opel moving again. Immediately the yellow Lancia pulled out and began trailing him at a respectable distance.

The next place on his list was one he'd already tagged as probably the most promising. Located under the shadow of the high bulk of San Salvatore, the Garage Stefano had been used regularly by Bullen Thoms for car hires.

The yellow Lancia pulled in again, further down the street, when Laird stopped at the Garage Stefano's forecourt. For the moment he ignored it. The driver had seen enough already; a little more wouldn't make much difference.

The Garage Stefano's car rental office was at one side of the service station area. A young girl attendant listened to him, gave a slightly puzzled nod, then asked him to wait. She went out, and soon the door opened again. A small man came in, wearing grubby white overalls. He had a large black moustache and was wiping his hands on a rag.

"*Signore.*" He gave Laird a quick, sharp-eyed inspection. "*Prego* . . . how can I help you?" He thumbed towards the window, at the Garage Stefano sign in the forecourt. "I am Stefano—Stefano Manotto. There is a bank that might have different views, but I own this place."

"I asked your young woman if she remembered a customer from England, a Signor Thoms," Laird said. "He mentioned this garage."

"*Sì.*" The little garage proprietor forced a wary smile. "How is Signor Thoms?"

"In good health," lied Laird. "He told me he has rented your cars several times."

"Most times he has been here, I think." The little man used an oil-stained finger to scratch an edge of his bristling moustache. "*Sì*, Signor Thoms is a good customer."

"But maybe not the easiest?" suggested Laird slyly.

Stefano chuckled. "Things have to be very right for him, *signore.*"

"I know." Laird put just the right degree of sympathy behind the words. He leaned his hands on the desk, which was the main piece of furniture in the room. "When did you see him last?"

"Three, maybe four weeks ago, Signor—ah—"

"My name is Morris." After the first lie, the others came more easily. "I might be interested in renting. The same kind of arrangement."

"*Buono.*" The little garage owner nodded easily. "I can rent car, or car and driver—Signor Thoms has done both."

"And driver?" Laird raised an eyebrow. "Where was he going? Somewhere special?"

"The market at Luino, over the border. Then down to visit his friend Signor Stassen, at the Villa Alton." The man chuckled. "I drove him myself that day, so I could say I've seen that house."

"What happened at the market?"

"I waited in the car; he bought things—he came back with a suitcase, and it was heavy. I had to lift it into the car."

"Then you dropped it off at the Villa Alton?" guessed Laird.

"*Sì.*" The garage owner blinked. "But—"

Laird had heard what he wanted. He moved away from it fast.

"Any idea why he came to you the first time?" he asked casually.

"I was recommended," said Stefano proudly. "He was sent to me by Signora Manton—an important lady here in Lugano." Beaming, he went towards the door, opened it, and beckoned. "*Prego* . . . let me show you something."

Laird followed him out into the gradually fading sunlight. They walked across the service station forecourt, past the pumps, then round to a workshop yard at the rear. The yard was filled with large trucks, parked side by side, nose to tail. At a rough count, Laird guessed there had to be at least forty of them. They looked new; they were all Fiats; they were all painted white with the Ticino canton colours of red and blue a vivid splash on every cab door.

"You know what these are, Signor Laird?" The little garage owner eyed him expectantly. "The trucks for the Relief Fund expedition—and Garage Stefano is where all have had their final servicing. Signora Manton said no one could do it better." A rueful twinkle showed in his eyes. "Better—or cheaper. But as she says, *pazienza* . . . it's all for charity."

"Slow down," said Laird, bewildered. He looked at the trucks again, seeing their thick, heavy-duty tyres, the extra roll-bars over the driver's cabs, the additional fuel tanks fitted under their chassis frames. Most were container vehicles, but there were a few with high canvas sides and a handful were tanker vehicles. "What Relief Fund? What expedition?"

"For refugees, Signor Laird." He was eager and enthusiastic. "For those poor devils starving in East Africa—haven't you seen them on TV, all skin and bone, empty stomachs like balloons? The whole Ticino has raised money for this convoy. Every vehicle has a full load—food, medicine, blankets. We have paid for the trucks, so they can stay out there. The drivers are volunteers." He gestured explosively. "In two days time these trucks parade at the town square, then leave—and I promise you, Lugano will give them a real send-off."

"How much is Elsa Manton involved?" asked Laird.

Stefano didn't notice his use of the woman's first name. He simply beamed again.

"She has done things here, she has done things there. *Ecco* . . . she is a marvellous woman." He chuckled. "Good-looking too, Signor Laird. When she was younger, I think—" He put finger and thumb together and winked.

"Maybe I should meet her," said Laird.

"Why not, if you know Signor Thoms? You have a mutual friend." The little man stuck his hands in his pockets. "You know the Via Nassa, with the jewellery stores?"

Laird nodded.

"The Relief Fund has an office further along, an empty shop. She is there most afternoons."

"I might do that." Laird walked towards the trucks, then inspected a few in the front rows. Containers were locked and sealed, the high-sided trucks had their canvas sides padlocked down. It was the same with the tanker trucks, the convoy's travelling fuel supply.

"These supplies—the blankets, medicines, the food—where were they loaded?"

"I don't know, *signore*. My job was just to make sure the trucks were serviced." The garage owner glanced round as a shout came from behind them. The woman attendant waved and beckoned him. "If you're interested, ask them at the Via Nassa—they welcome visitors, then empty their wallets."

He nodded goodbye and hurried off. Laird walked along another of the lines of trucks. They weren't new, but they'd been thoroughly reconditioned. As a convoy they would carry a payload of several hundred tons.

Blankets, food, medicines? Could it be so simple? Tight-lipped, he went back to the Opel and got behind the wheel. When he checked the driving mirror, the yellow Lancia was still parked along the street.

Starting the coupe, he eased it out of the parking slot. The road behind was clear of other traffic. Swiftly Laird flicked the gear lever into reverse, then kicked the accelerator to the floor.

Tyres screaming, the Opel rocketed backward down the tarmac. He braked, stopped it level with the Lancia, was out, round, and had wrenched open the other driver's door before the startled occupant could move.

"Out, Jo-Jo!" He grabbed the white-faced night clerk by the throat of his sweatshirt, jerked him bodily out of his seat, then slammed him back against the door pillar. "All right—why?"

"Please, Signor Laird—" The tubby night clerk cringed against the car, licking his lips. "I meant no harm."

"But you've been following me." Laird yanked him closer.

"*Sì.*" Jo-Jo managed a frightened nod.

"Why?"

"It was through my brother, Signor Laird—the one who works for the *polizia*, on their night switchboard." The man swallowed as Laird tightened his grip. "I told you about him—"

"Go on."

"*Si.*" Jo-Jo looked close to tears. "A man came to see me. He didn't tell me his name, Signor Laird, and he was not Swiss. But my brother said he had been told this man has high-placed friends— that whatever I did, you would come to no harm."

"That helps," said Laird. He released the night clerk as a car went past, the driver giving them a curious glance. "When did he come to you?"

"Yesterday—before you arrived in Lugano." Jo-Jo wiped a shaking hand across his mouth and watched Laird with apprehensive eyes. "I contact him through my brother, *signore*. But not any more, I swear it. *Finite . . .* I am not made for this kind of thing."

"Stick to chess," said Laird. "That's enough excitement for you, believe me."

Jo-Jo nodded earnestly.

"And pass on one more message through your brother—from me. Tell whoever is paying you that he can either meet me or get off my back."

"*Si.*" Jo-Jo forced a weak attempt at a smile. "*Grazie*, Signor Laird. I will do that, I promise."

Leaving him, Andrew Laird got back behind the wheel of Katie Holly's Opel and set it moving. Glancing in the rear mirror, he saw the night clerk still standing disconsolately by the roadside.

His mouth tightened. He'd been right—he was being watched, somehow he was being used. The way the night clerk had been contacted, even before he reached Lugano, was just part of it. He thought of Katie Holly. Did she know anything more than she'd told him? No, he dismissed the notion as unlikely.

Unlikely. It came back again. Unlikely, but not impossible—not the way everything else was shaping up, not now, when he had to figure out how a charity relief fund and a convoy of trucks fit in with all that had gone before them.

He found a parking space for the car in a side street near the Via Nassa, and walked from there through the usual jostling crowds of shoppers, past the glittering jewellery stores and the spotlit boutique windows.

The Relief Fund office wasn't hard to find. He must have walked past at least once before without noticing the small corner shop with handwritten posters on the windows and a painted banner above the door.

Laird went in. The front of the shop was laid out as an exhibition —enlarged, harrowing photographs of what famine could mean in Africa, maps of the affected areas, graphs showing money raised and what it would purchase. Next came a sales area, filled with donated goods of every kind. Then, at the back, there was the office area where two women were tapping busily at typewriters.

Neither of them was Elsa Manton. He cursed under his breath in disappointment, took another look around, then stopped short.

Three large paintings hung side by side on one wall, all on their own. The middle painting was an abstract swirl of yellow and light blue clouds with that winged butterfly trapped dark red in the centre—the same abstract he'd seen on the magazine cutting Miguel Holly had shown him in London, the flawed heart of a diamond.

Laird went over, raised an eyebrow at the amount on the price tag beneath it, then saw the firm signature "E. Manton" on the bottom right of the canvas. The same signature was on all the others, and any of them would have set him back several months' pay.

"*Permette* . . . may I help you, *signore?*" asked a voice.

He turned. It was one of the women who had been working in the office area. She was young, well dressed; her dark hair smartly styled, a broad wedding band among the rings on her fingers.

"I'm just looking." He smiled at her. "I like the paintings, but I can't afford them."

She gave a sympathetic pout with her lips. "Then maybe something else, *signore?* It's a good cause. If you look at the photographs of these people—"

"I heard you'd finished, that your convoy was ready to go."

"*Sì.*" The young woman nodded cheerfully. "The day after to-morrow. But we can always use more money, maybe get more cargo on the ship before she sails from Genoa."

So it was Genoa. Laird had more or less guessed it would have to be. The north Italian port was certainly as close to Switzerland as any other major harbour on the Mediterranean. From Lugano the truck convoy would have a simple autoroute journey to Milan; then another motorway link could carry it straight on from there to the sea.

"Do you know the name of the ship?" he asked casually.

"The *Volsella*—I can show you a photograph." A hand on his arm, she led Laird over to one of the displays and pointed. "That's her. Do ships interest you, Signore?"

"They're a hobby." He bent to peer at the glossy print. The *Volsella*, pictured leaving a harbour somewhere, was a reasonably modern, medium-sized cargo ship. Probably about ten thousand tons, needing a crew of about twenty, she was flying the Panamanian flag in the photograph. From what he could see of her layout, from heavy lift cargo derricks to her island bridge aft, she could handle container or heavy vehicle cargo with equal ease.

He sucked his lips. Ships like the *Volsella* also had a dry-hull insurance value running into millions.

"*Grazie.*" He glanced up at his guide. "She's certainly the kind of ship you need."

"We take advice." She nodded wisely, then brightened, looking past him. "Wait, maybe we can talk more about those paintings." She raised her voice. "Signora Manton—we have someone interested in your paintings."

Elsa Manton was standing at an open door at the rear of the shop. Still in the cream linen skirt and jacket outfit Laird had seen her wearing earlier, a handbag slung over one shoulder by its strap, the blond Austrian widow was obviously about to leave. She came over with a patient, slightly patronising smile.

"But is he interested enough to buy?" she asked casually. She considered Laird with some care and seemed to reach a decision. "We close here for good tomorrow—everything has to go. So don't worry too much about the price. We'd haggle a little."

"I'd have to haggle a lot," countered Laird without rancour. At close quarters, he decided to revise his estimate of Elsa Manton's age from early to late forties. She almost matched him in height—and probably in weight. He gestured towards the paintings. "Have I got it right—that abstract is a diamond?"

She shaped a slight, surprised frown, but nodded.

"I saw another one like it once—not so good, but the same idea." Laird stuffed his hands in the pockets of his denim jacket and nodded, wisely. "Do you know someone in the diamond trade?"

"Yes." She hesitated, then glanced at her wrist-watch. "I'm sorry, but I'm late for an appointment. Could you come back tomorrow?"

"It wouldn't be easy." Laird took a casual half-stop, which blocked her escape. "You know, I really like that painting."

"Then come back tomorrow. I have to leave, I—" She stopped there as the shop door opened, glanced round, and gave a murmur of relief.

Paul Stassen's dark-haired chauffeur was standing in the open doorway, staring at Laird, disbelief in his eyes. Stassen was behind him, trying to push him aside.

Laird's mouth dried as the dark-haired man growled a warning to Stassen at the same time as his hand dived into his jacket. The shop lights glinted on the blued metal of a gun. The two Relief Fund women had gone from their desks; he could hear their voices somewhere further back, but that was no help.

That left Elsa Manton. She might be big, but she was off guard. He grabbed her by the shoulders, spun her round, and threw her bodily at the two men. She yelped as they collided heavily enough for the dark-haired man to be knocked sprawling, Stassen left to grab her as she fell.

Laird ran past them before they could recover. The white Mercedes was parked outside, and he began sprinting in the opposite direction.

A dark blue Ford car started up ahead of him. It began moving, and the front passenger door swung open.

"Get in," yelled a voice in English. "Quickly."

He did, and the car gathered speed while he was still closing the door. They roared past Paul Stassen as he came out of the charity shop, took the shop corner in a squealing turn, then shaved past a line of parked cars in the narrow side-street. Bottoming hard on a pothole, the Ford swung right at the next corner.

"Hold on," said the man at the wheel. He spoke with a faint accent and twisted a grin at Laird. "Better make sure. Okay, Mr. Laird?"

They snaked through two more side-streets, climbed a steep, broad stretch of road, then swung off again. His driver gave a satisfied grunt, took his foot off the accelerator, flicked the gear lever into neutral, and let the car coast to a halt. They were above

Lugano, near the railway station. It was dusk, and the lights were coming on along the lakeside.

"Thanks." Laird settled back in his passenger seat and looked at the Ford's driver. He was stockily built, about forty, with short, prematurely grey hair and a raw-boned face. He wore a dark blue blazer, matching trousers, and an open-necked shirt. His right hand, resting lightly on the steering wheel, had no tip to its middle finger. "Not that it matters, but who the hell are you?"

"You sent me a rude message through our mutual friend Jo-Jo." The man kept his hand on the wheel and gave Laird a sideways glance. "What happened there was my fault, not his—agreed?"

"Agreed."

"Good." The man produced cigarettes, put one between his lips, and pressed the dashboard lighter. "Introductions, I suppose." He stopped as the lighter popped out, used it to light his cigarette, returned it to the socket, then reached into his inside jacket pocket. "Here."

Laird took the folded warrant card, dropped it into his lap, and read it in the fading light. Inspector Willi Dortman, temporarily attached to Interpol, was identified as a West German *Grenzschutzgruppe 9* police officer. He gave Dortman a quick, sideways glance. G.S.G. 9 was the West Germans' elite anti-terrorist squad, the same people who'd won their spurs ending the Mogadishu airliner hijack, people who weren't used without reason.

"This as well. It matters." A second pass was tossed across. "I know a lot about you, Mr. Laird. Maybe it's time you had your turn."

The second pass was also in Dortman's name, but issued by NATO military security. Dortman took both back and tucked them away. He took a long draw on his cigarette, let the smoke out slowly, then looked deliberately at Laird.

"I didn't set you up for this, Mr. Laird." His heavy shoulders shaped a shrug. "I knew what was happening, but that's all. Your own security people in London are the people to blame—they even scared the underwear off some funny little man called Morris. Your boss, right?"

"My boss," agreed Laird grimly.

"You don't look happy." Dortman took another puff at his cigarette and sighed. "I don't blame you. But listen—you've achieved more in a few days than my people have managed in as many months. You've been"—he paused and frowned—"what's the word?"

"A useful idiot?"

Dortman laughed. "No. Something else—yes, a catalyst. Things happen around you."

"Try explaining it," suggested Laird bleakly.

"The beginning was Bullen Thoms." Dortman scowled at the Ford's dashboard. "His name came up in Interpol criminal intelligence reports—not that stupid coffee fraud, more serious things."

"Like what?"

"He met people on the European terrorist fringe." Dortman shrugged. "We knew one of the men who killed him, one of the men who died in London. But we didn't know about Switzerland, or Lugano—not till you pointed us that way, with the diamonds. The diamonds linked with drugs, the drugs meant—" He sighed and shook his head. "I got here just ahead of you, Mr. Laird. So far the Swiss are diplomatically ignoring my existence. Any help is unofficial; I think they wish we'd all go away. But again, you got on to this Villa Alton just ahead of me—"

"What about Stassen?" asked Laird.

"He's on file. He served his apprenticeship as a mercenary in the Congo, in his teens; he was big trouble until a few years ago—then we thought he died. You met his dark-haired friend?"

Laird nodded.

"Danny Terras. He likes killing."

"He was at Zürich." Laird looked out at the gathering night. The sky had clouded over, the lake was a dark grey blanket. "Someone fell under a train."

"An Englishman. The autopsy report says he was stabbed first." Dortman wound down his window and threw away what was left of his cigarette. "You've been spotted, Mr. Laird. You can pull out now and try to get that Holly girl to do the same—we didn't know those damned fools at C.S.O. would send her in."

"Or?"

Dortman grinned. "Or we talk, you stay around, you keep stirring things up, and I make damn sure I keep both of you safe."

Laird stayed silent for a moment, knowing the sensible thing was to get out but remembering the rest.

"One question," he said slowly, "what's the bottom line?"

"With Paul Stassen involved, anything between a revolution and World War Three." Dortman looked at him carefully. "You'll stay?"

Laird nodded. They shook hands.

CHAPTER SEVEN

It was an hour later, the moon showing fitfully between clouds, before Andrew Laird was driven back into Lugano. He left the Interpol man's car two streets away from the Hotel Orchidea, walked the rest of the way, and went in to find Jo-Jo on duty at the reception desk.

"*Buona sera.*" The plump night clerk gave him a quick, nervous smile, scurried to hand over Laird's room key, then tried to make a fast retreat.

"Come here." Laird beckoned and considered him grimly. "I've spoken to your friend. He'll be in touch with you, or maybe you'll hear from your brother. We've agreed to a change of rules. You understand?"

Jo-Jo nodded anxiously. The chess board on his desk hadn't been touched.

Laird walked up to his second-floor room; once inside, he crossed to the window and looked down at the busy lakeside. He pursed his lips. Dortman had quizzed him closely about everything that had happened but hadn't volunteered much in return—except to say that it had been mainly luck he'd been outside the Relief Fund shop, that he'd gone there following Paul Stassen.

The whole situation was changing in a radical, dangerous way. Inspector Willi Dortman's arrival on the scene was an additional, in some ways welcome complication. But when Dortman offered guarantees, how much were they really worth?

It might be best not to have to find out.

He'd arranged to meet Katie Holly in the Orchidea's bar. Laird showered, changed into the grey suit he'd travelled in from London —the only suit he had with him—and a clean white shirt and dark grey tie. Then he went downstairs again. The hotel dining room had opened, the bar was quiet, and he ordered a whisky and water, then took his drink over to a corner table.

Katie Holly appeared promptly at eight. She was in a bottle-green-coloured velvet dress, sleeveless, with a mandarin neck, a narrow curl of silver embroidery around the waist. She dropped the coat she was carrying over the back of a spare chair, then sat opposite him.

"You look good," he told her.

"I damn well should." She was pleased but made a joke of it. "When I bought this dress, I wasn't robbed—I was sandbagged."

It was the first time he'd seen her wearing a dress instead of trousers. She had good legs, which he'd somehow expected. The cut of the smooth green velvet emphasised her firm breasts and the slim waist, the total young female animal quality of her figure. Her diamond pendant sparkled at her throat, as he'd expected. But the little glass-eyed mountain goat he'd bought her was pinned cheekily to the left side of her dress.

A waiter came over. Katie ordered a martini, and Laird waited until her drink arrived, then raised his own glass in a toast.

"To glass-eyed goats," he suggested.

"I like goats." She sipped her drink, then placed the glass carefully on the table. "You were right about going out to that airstrip."

"Did they buy your flying lessons story?"

She nodded, a twinkle in her eyes. "I got a free demonstration flight round the lake. Ever tried to tell a pilot to take his hand off your knee?"

"Not that I can remember," said Laird.

"It's different." Her mood changed abruptly. "Paul Stassen gives them plenty of charter work—they reckon at least one four-seat aircraft charter a week over the last three months. Sometimes he's flying out, the Manton woman with him now and again. But at least as often they've picked up 'business guests' and flown them into Lugano, round-trip style."

"Anything special about them?"

"My friendly pilot said some were fairly rough at the edges."

"How about cargo?"

"Nothing bigger than an overnight bag. Usually it's air-taxi stuff, linking with international flights into Geneva or Zürich, though

Stassen has used them for longer trips." She paused, a glint in her eyes. "That includes a few to Amsterdam."

"Then back with a pocketful of diamonds?"

"Maybe." She took a longer sip from her drink. "We could have a chance to find out. Stassen has a plane booked to fly to Geneva tonight and to collect two passengers coming in from Amsterdam. He'll meet them at the airstrip."

"When do they go back again?"

"Tomorrow sometime." Katie Holly paused, puzzled, looking at him. "You don't seem wildly excited. What's wrong?"

"New problems." Laird spread his hands flat on the table. "Stassen knows I'm here—and we've got company, a German named Dortman from Interpol. Dortman knows about me; he knows about you."

She frowned. "And wants us out?"

"He wants you out; he wants me as bait. He thinks things could get rough."

"Hard luck, Herr Dortman." Twin, angry spots of colour showed on her cheeks; her nostrils flared a little. "I'm here till Central Selling wants me to move." She glared at him with a sudden suspicion. "What did you say to him?"

"That you'd tell him to go to hell." Willi Dortman had admitted it would probably be that way but had still asked him to try. He'd tried. "Dortman meant well."

"Most traditionalist males do." She sighed; then her mood thawed. "Don't worry—if the wrong things happen, I disappear fairly quickly. Now do I get to hear the rest?"

He told her, starting with his own story, followed by the way Dortman had come to the rescue. She asked a probing question now and again, particularly when he told of his talk with Dortman on the hill above the town; then she chewed her lip and stayed silent for a moment when he'd finished.

"So you know about a ship," she said at last. "A ship at Genoa, and this relief fund convoy—now you've got to fit them to the rest of it?"

Laird nodded. Telling her, keeping to a tightly factual account, had helped here and there. He could pull some things more into perspective.

"You didn't tell him about Bernardo and Anna?" Katie had been doing her own thinking.

He shook his head. "There's a chance he already knows, through London. But if he doesn't, why drag them into it?" He saw she'd finished her drink. His own glass was empty, and he signalled the bar waiter for another round. "Has Bernardo come up with anything more?"

"Not yet."

"How about your Paris office?"

"They say they've no gem cutter named Schmidt on file who would match the description from here." She lowered her voice to a murmur as two couples settled noisily at a table beside them. "The diamond in the thumbnail bit helps more. They've about a score of possibles; they know what some are doing and where; they're checking on the rest."

The waiter returned with their drinks, then moved on to the next table. Katie didn't touch her glass for a moment.

"Stassen knows you're here; this hired nasty Danny Terras is around too—that means we forget the Casino Rosa tonight."

"I'd put it the other way round, say tonight is now our best chance," said Laird quietly. "You say Stassen will be at the airstrip. Terras will probably be with him."

She considered, fingering the glass-eyed brooch for a moment. Then she nodded.

"As long as we eat first—then look in on Bernardo and Anna before we go. I promised I would."

"Right." He was glad it was settled. "Your choice where we go."

"I like you, Andrew," she said demurely. "You treat women right. Finish that drink, will you?"

He'd given her back her car keys, he'd told her where he'd left the Opel coupe, but Katie Holly decided they should walk. It was only a few minutes from the hotel into the old quarter, along some narrow, cobbled streets which were busy enough and well enough lit to wipe away any background worries in Laird's mind.

The restaurant she chose didn't look much from the outside. One gable wall of the building was propped up by heavy wooden beams; the rest was old stonework painted white with narrow windows and a door which creaked when it opened. But once inside there was warmth and attentive waiters, crisp white table linen and soft lighting. A piano was being played in one corner; every table seemed occupied.

Laird let Katie do the talking. She had a brief, murmured exchange in rapid Italian, first with one waiter then with another, and their apologetic smiles changed to grins.

They were installed at a table in an alcove. The scarred, blackened roof beams overhead had got that way with age, not chemical treatment; a row of copper utensils decorating one wall would have been an antique collector's delight; some of the cutlery in front of Laird was solid silver.

They ordered from a handwritten menu, decided on a bottle of dry Frascati, and by the time it arrived Laird had heard enough of the buzz of conversation around to know they had to be the only foreigners in the place.

Their food quickly followed the wine. Laird had a *risotto* of beef and marrow, rice, onions, and saffron as his main course. Katie was presented with an equally massive platter of *cotoletta milanese* and made no complaint. Every time Laird glanced up, a waiter seemed to be hovering within sight.

"How did we manage this table?" he asked.

"I told them I had my first real birthday party here, when I was five." She winked. "It's true. I stuffed myself rotten, then threw up as we left—but I didn't remind them of that part."

He discovered she had once owned a sailing dinghy; she got him to confess a secret ambition to try microlight flying. Suddenly he found himself telling her the story of the one diamond ring he'd ever bought in his life—an engagement ring for a woman who had changed her mind. She'd pawned the ring to raise money for her air fare to Canada, flying out with another man—but she'd mailed Laird the pawn ticket.

Katie tried to look sympathetic, failed, and shook with silent laughter for a moment. Then, still smiling, she murmured under her breath.

"Like to say that again?" suggested Laird.

"Just an old saying about diamonds—they chase nightmares, shield the wearer against magic, bring courage in battle."

Laird rubbed a hand across his jaw, considering the diamond pendant she was wearing.

"What about that one? Does it work?"

"I wouldn't rely on it. But I know what my father does any time he moves house—he touches each corner of the new home with a diamond. It's an old superstition about keeping out the Devil."

They finished the meal with thin slivers of cheese and celery, washed down with coffee and the last of the Frascati. Laird braced himself as the bill arrived, discovered it was considerably less than he'd expected, paid; then most of the restaurant staff seemed to find time to fuss around Katie and help her with her coat as they left.

Outside the night had become cold and the sky was clear. Katie suddenly took his arm and huddled against him for warmth.

Bernardo Garri's shop and home was only a few cobbled streets away, and they began walking, stopping a couple of times to look at boutique display windows, a mutual, unspoken agreement forbidding any mention of the harsh reality waiting across Lake Lugano.

Laird noticed it first, the faint, acrid scent of smoke and burning. It grew stronger, a flashing blue light reflected on the walls of a building; then Katie's grip had tightened anxiously on his arm, and they were both hurrying.

They turned a corner. Katie gave a horrified gasp, and they stopped. Bernardo Garri's little shop was just ahead—or what was left of it. Two fire tenders, police cars, and an ambulance filled the narrow roadway. Hoses still snaked across the cobbles; a spotlight played on the charred wood and broken glass remnants of the shop front; smoke drifted in the air; a small crowd of onlookers stood gaping.

The rear doors of the ambulance were open; someone lay inside on a stretcher. The attendant climbed down and elbowed his way past a group of firemen and police as another figure was assisted out of the shop doorway. Smoke-blackened, obviously dazed, leaning heavily on the arm of a fireman, Anna Garri was assisted towards the ambulance.

"Oh, my God." Katie Holly let go of Laird's arm and rushed forward.

A policeman stopped her. Laird heard her shout Anna Garri's name, but it was too late. Gently the woman was helped into the ambulance. The attendant got aboard, the doors closed, and the ambulance pulled away into the night with its siren wailing and emergency lights flashing.

Pushing forward through the onlookers, the remnants of smoke stinging his eyes, Laird reached Katie. She finished talking to the policeman and turned towards him, a mixture of disbelief and despair on her face.

"They don't know what happened, Andrew. Someone saw flames; then the whole shop seemed to go up—"

"How about Anna and Bernardo?"

"Anna will be all right." They think she's suffering from shock and smoke as much as anything. Bernardo"—she bit her lip—"they found him in the front shop, unconscious. He's badly burned."

"Do you know where they've been taken?"

She nodded, her face briefly in shadow as the spotlight behind them switched off, then came on again.

"The Ospedale Civico—it's about five minutes from here." She drew a deep breath. "I'm sorry, Andrew, but I'll have to go there. Anna is going to need help; I've got to find out how Bernardo is."

Laird looked past her as some debris crashed down from the floor above the burned-out shop. Whatever had happened had been swift and furious. He knew enough about fires to have his own, immediate suspicions, and he wanted to see Willi Dortman, talk to the G.S.G. inspector. But it was his fault that Dortman didn't know about Bernardo Garri and his wife—so why should Dortman be anywhere near?

"We'll get your car." He touched her arm. "I'll come with you."

She nodded gratefully, and they started back the way they'd come. They reached the corner again, and suddenly they weren't alone. A figure appeared from a doorway ahead. Swift footsteps approached from behind; then the unmistakable muzzle of a gun jammed hard and low against Laird's back. Someone else had grabbed Katie, and there was a quick scuffle as she was held. On ahead, the man from the doorway glanced around, acting as a lookout.

"Tell that damn woman to behave," said a soft, cold voice in his ear. "The same goes for you, Laird. He wants you alive, but it doesn't have to be that way."

Katie had a hand clasped over her mouth, one arm twisted viciously behind her back, and she was staring at him. Laird gave a slight, warning shake of his head. She tried to nod; then she stopped struggling.

"That's better," said the same voice with a wisp of brittle amusement. "No one stays lucky for ever—and you've had your share."

Laird looked round, slowly, so there could be no misunderstanding. Danny Terras was behind him, his thin, pinched face empty of emotion, his sharp eyes bright and restless. Paul Stassen's darkhaired lieutenant looked as though he might easily kill them both without compunction.

"I wondered who'd been playing with matches," said Laird with disgust. "Did you have to burn down Garri's place?"

"We taught them a lesson—that's all. I thought we'd stay close for a spell, to see what happened." Terras almost chuckled. "So we get you as a bonus—that saves some time." The gun muzzle dug viciously. "Move. You make trouble, she gets it. She makes trouble, you get it. You both understand?"

They were hustled a short distance down the street, then into a darkened lane where a small van was parked. They were pushed into the rear in a way that had Katie swearing quietly and angrily; then Danny Terras and one of his men climbed in after them. As the van doors closed, a roof light was switched on. Terras gripped a Mauser pistol, watching both of them carefully.

"Make sure of them, Lucci," he ordered.

His companion tucked the small revolver he'd been holding into his waistband, then scrambled forward. He frisked Laird quickly and expertly, swung him round, and in another few seconds Laird's wrists had been tied behind his back with what felt like strong, thin fishing line. He repeated the process with Katie but taking his time, grinning. White with anger, she spat in his face as he touched her again.

"Bitch." The man cuffed her casually across the mouth, then glanced at Terras.

"Leave her," ordered Terras in a bored voice.

The man scowled, wiped his face on his sleeve, then knocked on the metal partition between them and the driver's compartment. The van started up noisily and began moving.

"Where are you taking us?" asked Laird.

"On a boat trip—no charge, Mr. Laird." Danny Terras settled himself comfortably on the van floor, the Mauser resting across one knee. "Enjoy it." He glanced at Katie. "The same goes for you, lady. If I have to shoot, you're just as much on the firing line—whoever the hell you are."

The van rumbled on, but not for long. They slowed. The vehicle lurched for a moment; then they had stopped. A fist rapped twice on the partition, from the driver's side. Terras gave a grunt of satisfaction.

"Same rules," he warned.

The van doors opened, they were pushed out, and Laird's feet crunched on loose gravel. They were somewhere near the north edge of the town, on the lakeside, the rest of Lugano a glittering curve, the brilliant plumes of the floodlit fountain jets like small feathers in the distance.

The man named Lucci shoved him hard and almost sent him sprawling. He turned and followed Terras and Katie along a small wooden jetty to where a small launch was moored. He saw the name *Alton I* on the bow and remembered the last time he'd seen it, moored to the private jetty near the Casino Rosa.

"Get in," ordered Terras. He pointed at Laird. "You first."

Awkwardly, cursing the way his hands were tied, Laird scrambled down. Lucci jumped after him, landed in a way that sent the little hull rocking at her moorings, then grabbed Katie as Terras shoved her in after them. Terras paused, waved towards the stopped van, and the driver answered with a brief wink of his headlights. The van turned and drove off; the launch engine barked to life and throbbed exhaust as Lucci thumbed its starter button, and Terras dropped easily into the cockpit after casting off the mooring lines.

"Take her out," said Terras. He gestured towards the stern. "You two, stay back there."

He snapped his fingers at Lucci, was handed a small hand-held radio with a black stub of aerial, and began speaking into it while the boat swung round in the water. A reply crackled back; he spoke again, then tossed the radio aside.

"Got the welcome mat arranged?" asked Laird.

"All the welcome you're going to get," said Danny Terras. He bared his teeth at Katie in what was meant to be a grin. "Maybe I can manage something better for you."

"Like you managed for Bernardo Garri and his wife?" she suggested contemptuously.

He shrugged and took a half-step nearer in the close confines of the cockpit area. Laird gauged the distance, braced himself against the stern combing, and kicked for the man's gun hand.

Terras was fast, too fast. He sidestepped the kick, the Mauser swung, and the barrel smashed against the side of Laird's head. Then the gun had moved again and was jammed under Katie's chin.

"Behave, or you're next. Now sit down, both of you."

Dazed from the blow, Laird had to slump down and was vaguely aware of Katie Holly trying to support him. Terras retreated to join Lucci, and the launch gathered speed. Bouncing and pitching, a white turbulence of wake behind her, she began heading out towards the Italian shore.

There was other night traffic on the lake, moving blobs of light that might have been tiny water beetles. They overtook one, a large, brightly lit boat on an evening cruise, music coming from her afterdeck, people waving from the rails. Lucci grinned, gave a blast on *Alton I*'s klaxon horn, and waved back.

"Damn him," said Katie tightly, her mouth close to Laird's ear, her voice almost lost under the roar of the launch's engines. "If he tries to paw me again, he'll get my teeth in his throat."

"No. Don't." Laird spoke hoarsely. His head still throbbed; he was glad of the fine, almost icy mist of spray in the air as the launch slammed on. "Take it, wait."

"Why?"

"Dortman." He forced the words. "They don't know about him. When he can't find us—"

"No talking." Danny Terras lurched over again and glared down at them. "Keep your mouths shut, both of you. Get lower down—out of sight. Now."

They obeyed and lay bundled together, Laird's face almost buried in Katie's hair.

He thought of Willi Dortman. How long would it be before Dortman realised something had happened? How quickly could the G.S.G. 9 man act? Time mattered. He and Katie might have a limited use, even a curiosity value to Paul Stassen and his people—but after that?

The launch bucked again, and a statistic he'd rather have forgotten forced its way into Laird's mind: Some parts of Lake Lugano were almost one thousand feet deep.

They were heading towards an area of bright lights on the Italian shore, and as she came nearer, the launch slowed and altered course. Terras growled another warning; then they were coming into the little bay where the Casino Rosa was located. Speed reduced to a crawl, the boat came close in towards the pier. Lucci shouted, a cheerful voice called back, and the launch swung away again, gathering speed.

"Italian customs check—always law-abiding, that's us." Terras winked at Lucci, who grinned. "They know us—we say hello, goodbye. Good arrangements, eh, Mr. Laird?"

Then they were ignored. The fast launch was near her destination, and in another minute they bumped against the Villa Alton's private landing stage. Lights came on, two men appeared, Laird and Katie Holly were hauled out of the launch and pushed across the planks to dry ground. One of the men stayed to secure the launch; the other took the lead with a large hand torch, and Terras and Lucci herded their two prisoners after him along the path towards the villa.

It was a short, steep climb. At the top, the Villa Alton stark and pale ahead with the central turret silhouetted in the moonlight, they had to wait until a gate in the high boundary fence was unlocked. It locked again once they were through.

"I'm impressed," said Laird sarcastically. "You should get a rebate on burglary insurance."

Terras grunted his amusement, but shoved him on again.

Beyond the fence, the path went through a stretch of overgrown shrubbery, then joined a driveway which led to the main door of the Villa Alton. Lights showed at the windows; the air held the scent of woodsmoke; an owl was hooting somewhere.

Their guide with the hand torch took them to the door, opened it, then disappeared. Pushed on, Katie and Laird entered a large, chilly, stone-flagged hallway lit by an old-fashioned metal chandelier. Terras thumbed them through an archway, tapped on a door, straightened himself a little as a voice barked a reply, then opened the door and led the way in, Lucci coming last.

Paul Stassen stared at them across the big, plainly furnished room, a look of annoyance twisting his broad face. He was standing with his back to a log fire which burned in a large stone hearth, the flames bright enough to reflect in his long, coppery hair, and he had company. A burly, bearded, startled-looking stranger in an ill-fitting business suit rose quickly from a chair and gave Stassen an anxious glance. Elsa Manton, curled comfortably on a couch, shaped a frown of surprise.

"Damn you for an idiot, Danny," said Stassen softly, scowling at Terras. "I didn't mean drag them straight in here."

"Sorry, Paul." Terras's thin features twisted apologetically; he turned quickly, grabbing Laird's arm.

"No, leave them," ordered Stassen with a resigned air. He caught Elsa Manton's slight, warning gesture in the direction of the bearded man, who was clutching a briefcase, and gave a quick, reassuring grunt. "No need to worry, captain—just a small misunderstanding."

The bearded man chewed his lip, then nodded. But he stayed standing.

Leaving his place by the fire, Paul Stassen crossed the room. He gave Terras a reassuring slap on the shoulder, gave an encouraging nod in Lucci's direction, then stopped in front of Laird and Katie.

"I know most things about you, Mr. Laird." His light blue eyes, small and cold, considered Laird dispassionately. "Enough, at any rate."

"I'm still catching up on you," said Laird.

"People try." Stassen switched his attention to Katie, and a trace of doubt showed on his broad face. "I'm not totally sure about the lady, but—yes, we'll remedy that."

Katie said nothing. In the background Elsa Manton chuckled.

"Take them somewhere, Danny. Check them over." Stassen beckoned Elsa Manton. "Elsa, you can help. Make sure of the girl— a woman's way, you understand?"

The blond woman nodded and got to her feet. But she glanced towards the bearded man.

"What about him?"

"I'm late already, Mr. Stassen," said the man eagerly. "It's a long drive back."

"We're almost finished," said Stassen. "Just a last couple of details to go." He paused, and a devil of amusement glinted briefly in his eyes. "Laird, you're interested in the *Volsella*, the Relief Fund ship. This is her master, Captain Walmer. He wants to get back to Genoa."

Horrified, the bearded captain almost dropped his briefcase.

"Mr. Stassen—" he protested.

"Be quiet," said Stassen wearily. "He knows the ship. You're the captain—it's no big deal." Turning, he nodded to Terras. "Move them. Elsa, get some help."

They were taken back out into the hallway. Elsa Manton called, and a fat woman in housekeeper's overalls waddled through from the rear of the house. They took Katie into one room, and Laird was shoved along to another.

His hands were cut free. Terras's automatic prodding him again, he was forced to strip, then shoved to one side. Stooping, Lucci pawed carefully through Laird's clothing and gathered everything that had been in his pockets into a neat pile.

"Finito." He looked up at Terras, nodded, then grinned at the tattoo marks on Laird's arms. "So—a *marinaio*, eh? I was a soldier once, a *caporale.*"

"Until he was caught stealing army stores," said Terras. The automatic pistol jerked again. "Against the wall. You know the way."

Lucci finished the body search with a coarse brutality that left Laird more coldly angry than he'd felt for a long time. They let him dress again, but kicked his coat to one side and kept his tie to loosely bind his wrists together again.

He was first back into the room where Paul Stassen was waiting. The *Volsella*'s captain had gone, and Stassen was standing in front of the log fire again, a drink in his hand. He set the glass down on a table, took the handkerchief-wrapped bundle from Lucci, glanced at Laird's passport and wallet, then discarded the rest as the door swung open again.

Katie was brought in by the fat housekeeper, who had a twist-grip on her right arm. Laird winced. Katie's dress was ripped at one shoulder, blood oozed from a gashed lip, and she was limping. Pushing in behind them, Elsa Manton was in a similar state of disarray and nursed her left arm.

"Trouble, Elsa?" murmured Stassen with barely hidden amusement.

"She was awkward." The blond woman pushed forward and dumped a small collection on the table beside Laird's items. "The little cow bites."

Katie swore at her. Stassen grinned, raked through the things which had been taken from her, found the Central Selling Organisation I.D. card, and pursed his lips for a moment while he studied it.

"Her clothing, the rest?"

"Mostly Paris labels, what I'd expect—nothing unusual."

"Good. Maria"—Stassen turned to the housekeeper—"you can go. But tell Signor Meihan I want him here, straight away."

The housekeeper nodded, shoved Katie over beside Laird, then left them. Crossing to a small bar cabinet, Elsa Manton poured herself a large brandy, then took a gulp from the glass before she sank down on her couch again.

"So—let's deal with you for the moment, Laird," said Stassen almost affably. "I haven't time to waste. I have to leave soon. But tell me this—why here, why Lugano? Did Bullen Thoms tell you more than I thought?"

"He just made some mistakes," said Laird.

"What kind?" demanded Stassen.

Laird shrugged. Talking a little could do no harm.

"Enough to point us to Lugano. Then we found he'd been collecting diamonds—but the mice had been at them."

Stassen blinked, understood, and swore under his breath.

"We made some mistakes too. He was one of them. I can think of another. I suppose you didn't really follow one of my people from London—a man who was on your flight to Zürich?"

Laird shook his head and Stassen shot a glare in Danny Terras's direction.

"That's why you had him killed?" asked Katie incredulously.

"He thought he'd been followed, and I was told," said Stassen unemotionally. "I left the decision to the man on the spot."

"Do you mind if I laugh?" asked Laird. He nodded at Terras. "I saw your rat-faced friend at Zürich; then I saw him here, and he led me to you."

Stassen stayed silent for a moment, thinking, his small eyes half-closed.

"Why were you at the Relief Fund shop?"

"Because I don't like some of the people running it." Laird met the half-closed eyes calmly. "Then you showed up, and that clinched it. You're using it as some kind of front—that convoy of trucks, that ship. There's another ship somewhere too, if Bullen Thoms told the truth."

Danny Terras gave a strangled curse, and Elsa Manton froze with the brandy glass not quite at her lips. Though he rode the surprise well, Paul Stassen's face hardened.

"You've been busy," he said softly. "But I don't think things would be this way if you knew everything."

"We were getting near."

"But not being very clever," said Stassen. "You blunder around Lugano asking about Bullen Thoms; the young woman and her friends go around making their own noises about diamonds—did you really imagine none of it would get back to me?"

Laird glanced at Katie. Neither of them answered.

"Elsa." Stassen turned. "What do you think?"

"They've been working on their own." She was positive. "The Swiss police don't know about them."

"Or you would have heard—that's certain." Stassen crossed to her and laid an affectionate hand against her cheek. She liked it, but Laird had a mental picture of an owner patting a favourite pet. Smiling, Stassen spared a moment to explain. "Elsa's police sources are very reliable. Like me, they think she is something special—and there are police wives sitting beside her on that Relief Fund committee."

"But there's still a problem." Elsa Manton frowned up at him. "They were sent here—"

"I haven't forgotten." Stassen nodded slowly. "But we only need a few days. Then we fade away, don't linger. Goodbye Lugano—the way we've always planned."

The door opened. The man who came in was slight in build, grey-haired, more than middle-aged, and had thin, pale, long-jawed features. He wore a dark suit with a grubby white shirt and a string-like dark tie, and he gave Stassen a nervous smile, showing large, yellowed, horse-like teeth.

"A little task, Johan." Stassen went over to the table, picked up Katie's I.D. card, and stuck it under the newcomer's nose. "This belongs to one of our visitors. How much does she matter?"

The tiny diamond set in the grey-haired man's thumbnail sparkled in the light as he took the card and peered at it.

"Our resident expert," said Stassen casually. "One of South Africa's finest—though they'd probably rather forget about you, eh Johan?" He chuckled. "Johan's talents have never been questioned, just the way he uses them."

Meihan gave a weak, dutiful smile, but he was staring at Katie.

"Well?" asked Elsa Manton.

"She matters," said Meihan unhappily. "Central Selling is like a trade union for the top diamond dealers."

Stassen drew a deep breath. "How would they get involved, for God's sake?"

"I warned you," said Meihan weakly. "These stones—"

"All right." Stassen cut him short. He glanced at his wrist-watch, then crossed to Katie. Taking her chin between finger and thumb, he forced her to look at him. "Well? What's the rest of it?"

She didn't answer and his grip tightened.

"Let her go," said Laird resignedly. "C.S.O. were told we'd found the Bullen Thoms diamonds. They knew I was on my way here; they sent her. That's all."

Stassen hesitated, scowling. Then Meihan made a nervous, attention-seeking noise at his side.

"Could—could I borrow this?" Meihan was clutching Katie's gold pendant with the single diamond in its centre. "It—well, it interests me."

"Damn you," said Katie. "My father gave me that."

"Take it," said Stassen.

"Go play with your toys, Meihan," said Elsa Manton contemptuously. "We're busy." She glanced at Stassen. "And behind schedule."

Stassen nodded. Blinking his thanks, Meihan took another hasty glance at Katie, then left the room. As the door closed, Danny Terras gave a derisive laugh, then thumbed at Laird and Katie.

"What do I do with them?"

"Make sure we don't lose them. They might be useful." Stassen frowned at Laird. "There's more I want to find out from you, Laird. But it'll have to be tomorrow." He gave a sardonic grin. "Life's a rat race right now."

Laird shrugged. "It looks like the rats are winning."

"And it's going to stay that way." Stassen refused to be riled. "Danny, keep them separate."

"Where?"

"Outside the house, somewhere visitors can't trip over them." Stassen made up his mind. "Use the old ice-house for Laird; put her in the empty storage loft above the garage. Move him first; we'll keep an eye on his little friend till you get back."

Andrew Laird was taken from the room, along a corridor, and through the kitchen quarters of the villa out into a cobbled back yard. He was halted in front of a small, windowless stone hut; the necktie was removed from his wrists; then, Terras guarding him, Lucci unlocked a heavy wooden door, reached in, and switched on a single electric light set in a bulkhead fitting in the ceiling.

"Inside," ordered Terras and shoved him forward. His pinched face shaped an unsympathetic leer. "Have a good night."

The door slammed shut; the key turned in the lock again. Andrew Laird heard the muffled sound of laughter from outside; then the men had gone. They'd left the light burning. He drew a deep breath and looked around his prison.

The door would have needed a battering ram, and there was nothing he could do about the lock. The walls were constructed of heavy stone blocks, cold to the touch, and the peaked roof was a combination of thick wooden beams and planks. But it was the floor level that mattered.

Stassen had called the place "the old ice-house," and it was the rough equivalent of similar relics Laird had seen in his native Scotland. A deep, well-like hole, lined with stone, occupied most of the space. In winters past he could picture horse-drawn sledges bringing blocks of ice down from the hills to fill it—ice that would supply the villa's needs for most of the summer months.

He grimaced at the overhead light. It hadn't been left burning for any humanitarian reasons. Without it, he might have fallen over that edge and been found dead at the bottom of that pit.

Exploring the rest of the cobwebbed, abandoned hut didn't take long. He found a few empty sacks lying in a corner and eyed them gratefully. The air was chill; it was likely to be a long, cold night; he was already shivering.

Gathering the sacks, making them up as a rough bed, he squatted down and pulled one over his shoulders. A new sound from outside, faint through the stone blocks, was an engine of some kind—boat or car, he had no way of knowing which. Paul Stassen must be on his way to the airstrip to meet his all-important visitors.

Katie Holly must have heard it too, in her own makeshift prison. Laird clenched his fists under the sacking. They'd given her a rough time; there was probably worse ahead.

But time, rough or otherwise, was the thing they needed most. Time—and the outside hope represented by Willi Dortman. So far Stassen hadn't pressed them too hard on their story, was still self-assured, secure in Elsa Manton's certainty that the Swiss authorities in Lugano knew nothing, confident that he could handle any other problems.

They'd be missed at the Hotel Orchidea, but hotel managements the world over were reluctant to make a fuss—and if a couple didn't occupy their individual beds for a night or so, the main reaction might be a few winks and nudges.

What else was left? Bernardo Garri and his wife were in no immediate position to do anything; Osgood Morris in London might curse and wonder why there was no contact; Katie's boss in Paris might do the same. But no immediate alarm bells would start ringing.

All he could do, all Katie could do, was wait. Some kind of chance might shape itself—and Paul Stassen would keep them alive as long as he thought they were useful.

It was as comforting a thought as Laird could find. He huddled down under the sacking and tried to sleep.

It seemed a long night. Andrew Laird slept fitfully, woke several times shaking with cold, and twice forced himself through a series of physical exercises to combat the chill. If it had been winter, he knew the temperature would probably have fallen low enough to bring the incipient dangers of hypothermia, the killer drowsiness, as his brain was starved of oxygen. As it was, he felt weak and his joints ached before faint lines of daylight began showing round the edges of his prison door.

Another long time passed before he heard voices and the door opened. Lucci and another man, a stranger armed with a shotgun, fetched him out into the bright sunlight of the courtyard and from there into the kitchen quarters. They let him use a small washroom, then allowed him to stand beside the heat of a big, old-fashioned kitchen range. The fat, wooden-faced housekeeper Maria silently gave him a mug of scalding coffee and a chunk of bread.

The two men watched him eat, stopped him when he tried to ask the woman about Katie, and pushed him on again.

"Up there, *Inglese.*" Lucci nodded towards a narrow, winding flight of stairs. "Signor Stassen doesn't like waiting."

It was a long climb, up into the central turret of the villa. At the top Lucci tapped on a door, opened it, and the two men herded Laird into a small room fitted out as a study. Stassen, dressed in a sweater and slacks, sat at a desk. Narrow window slits behind him gave a view out across Lake Lugano to the hills and mountains of Switzerland.

"Sit down," ordered Stassen, pointing at a chair placed in front of his desk.

Laird took the chair. Stassen looked tired; he hadn't shaved but seemed in good spirits. Opening a drawer, he took out a small automatic pistol and laid his hand on the desk with the pistol pointing towards Laird.

"So that we understand each other," he said softly, then glanced at his men. "Wait outside."

They backed out, the door closed behind them, and Stassen stifled a yawn.

"A late night, then an early morning." He grinned to himself. "I won't ask if you slept, Laird. This place isn't equipped for your kind of guest."

"What about Katie?" asked Laird.

"The lady seems well," said Stassen dryly. "Ill-tempered, some-

what abusive—but well. I talked to her here a few minutes ago."
Suddenly he slapped his free hand hard on the desk. "She wanted to
know about Garri and his wife. I'll tell you the same as I told her.
Garri is recovering. But he and his wife both know they have to
keep their mouths shut—particularly if they want to see either of
you two again. No one else seems worried; nothing has changed
from my viewpoint."

"Suppose it stays that way—what about us?" asked Laird unemotionally.

Stassen shrugged. "I don't know yet. That's an honest answer—"

"Or as honest as we'll get?"

Stassen gave a faint shrug. Reaching into the same drawer, he
brought out cigarettes and a lighter and lit a cigarette. The pistol in
his other hand didn't shift.

"Did you really try to blackmail Bullen Thoms?" he asked suddenly.

Laird shook his head.

"I didn't particularly believe it when he came here. That's why I
told my people it would be enough to—well, incapacitate you for a
spell."

"They tried," said Laird. "What about the photograph they
had?"

"Of you?" Stassen drew on his cigarette. "I had Thoms arrange
that." He shook his head. "My weakest link, Laird—but I'd call the
result limited damage." He paused. "How much do you know about
me?"

"Not a lot. I hadn't much chance."

"True." It amused the man. "And the Relief Fund convoy?"

"You're using it, somehow."

"True again." Stassen eyed him closely and seemed satisfied.
"The food, the medicine bought by the good people of the Ticino
canton will still get through—I'll simply use the opportunity."

"So you've extra cargo aboard the trucks?"

Stassen sighed impatiently but again seemed oddly pleased. He
gestured towards one of the turret window slits, away from the view
across the lake.

"Go over there, look out." He aimed the pistol significantly.
"Then come back."

Laird rose and went over. The turret window looked out on the rear of the Villa Alton, across the courtyard and the old ice-house, across a screen of high hedge. Beyond the hedge—he stiffened and stared. Covered in camouflage netting, but still visible from the turret viewpoint, he slowly counted the rows of big, white-painted trucks with blue and red Ticino badges on their doors. He stopped at twenty. There were still more.

"That's enough."

Stassen's voice brought him back to the chair, and he sat down again.

"Neat," he admitted wryly. "You'll slot them in?"

"The paperwork is arranged; the drivers will be my men." Stassen nodded. "The genuine convoy leaves from Switzerland; my trucks join it in Italy—all relief aid, and what port authority, loading or unloading, would think of interfering?"

"And two ships, so the real convoy doesn't get there first?" Laird didn't wait. Suddenly he knew the answer to the other question. "So you're gun-running?"

"There are more sophisticated descriptions," said Stassen almost lazily. "Thank you, Laird."

"For what?"

"For proving you didn't know before." Stubbing his cigarette in an ashtray, Stassen raised his voice, "Lucci—"

The door opened. Lucci and the other guard came in.

"Put him back," ordered Stassen.

"Will you need him again, *signore?*" asked Lucci. "Or the woman?"

"No." Stassen saw the quick, wolfish grin on the man's face. "I mean not today. Maybe tomorrow—don't damage the goods."

Lucci gave a disappointed nod.

He was taken back to the stone hut. The door slammed on him, the lock clicked. He heard his guards leave.

It was easy to curse, to give way to a sense of despair, and Andrew Laird did both. But only briefly; then it passed, and he fought a small personal battle to get back to rational thinking. All right, Paul Stassen had deliberately baited him along, tempted him with some of the things he wanted to know, had let him see the duplicate relief convoy—and had gained from Laird the one point he really wanted to be sure about.

It wasn't finished. Stassen still didn't realise the amount of background that had been gathered. Whatever happened next, there were people on the outside watching and waiting. But could they do enough, do it soon enough, to stop those substitute trucks and their loads from sailing—perhaps even getting through to their destination?

Laird put his mind to work again, trying to think in terms of quantities, of total tonnage. Willi Dortman had made a grim jest about "a small war," but depending on the type of weaponry those trucks carried, it might not be so small. It would certainly be bloody.

He gave up at last, a different thought in his mind, one that wouldn't go away.

What was happening to Katie Holly?

The day crawled on. He talked to himself; he walked clockwise then anti-clockwise round the ice-house pit; he counted the lines in the stone blocks; he got to know every nail hole in the rafter beams.

It was early afternoon when the door swung open. He was given another mug of coffee and a hunk of cold sausage on a plate.

The door closed again. It stayed that way another long time; then again the lock clicked, again the door swung back.

This time he had a visitor. He stared as the grey-haired, stooped figure of Johan Meihan came in. Meihan was alone, but just outside the doorway the same guard with the shotgun stood watching.

Laird had been sitting cross-legged on the pile of sacks. He got up slowly.

"And what the hell do you want?" he asked.

"I want to hear about diamonds, Mr. Laird," said Meihan loudly, almost fiercely. "The diamonds you found after Thoms was killed."

The man came nearer. A quick smile crossed his thin, nervous face. One hand was clenched.

"More important, Mr. Laird," his voice dropped to a whisper. "I want to help you out of here. Miss Holly said to get this, that you'd understand."

He opened his hand and showed Laird the little brooch that was a glass-eyed mountain goat.

CHAPTER EIGHT

It took more than a moment to realise what the man had said; then even the sight of the little brooch he'd bought at the Casino Rosa souvenir shop wasn't enough.

"I'm supposed to believe you?" asked Andrew Laird hoarsely.

"You must, Mr. Laird." Johan Meihan gave a quick, anxious glance over his shoulder at the open door and the lounging guard. "I managed to persuade Stassen that I should talk to you, but even this is a risk for all of us." He bit his lip. "Please, speak quietly."

"All right." Laird did as the man asked. "You work for Stassen. Why change sides like this?"

Meihan showed his yellowed teeth in a weary smile. "You may not understand—"

"Try me."

"Last night, in the villa, I saw that pendant with the diamond. Do you remember? I asked Stassen if I could borrow it—"

"Go on." Laird nodded.

The man sighed. "Mr. Laird, diamonds and precious stones have been my life as far back as I can remember. I have certain skills, certain talents. I am a craftsman, whatever else. So I can tell you this. There may be only one small diamond in that pendant, but the man who cut it, created it, makes me feel humble, a beginner." He shook his head in wry respect. "I couldn't put a value on that little stone, Mr. Laird, not in money terms. But it is a gift of love—a father's love for a daughter, expressed by a master craftsman."

"I've met him," said Laird.

"So have I. We were apprentices together." Meihan eyed him steadily. "His daughter also said you know very little about diamonds."

Laird nodded.

"Diamonds are a world of their own for those who understand

them." The slight, grey-haired man drew a deep breath. "To create a finished stone from a rough diamond, you—yes, you require a blend of mathematics and vision, geometry and skill. There are styles of cut—dozens of them, some for brilliance, others for depth, a few to hide reality. They have names like the Lisbon, the Holland Rose, the Cairo Star, the Old English. Or there are newer styles, like the American, with its higher crown and smaller table." He leaned forward earnestly. "Each is a fresh creation, a work of art. Do you follow me?"

"I'm trying." Laird glanced past him. The guard outside was lighting a cigarette. "What about Katie Holly's pendant?"

"This man Miguel Holly"—Meihan could only gesture his admiration—"with so small a diamond, he has taken the seventeenth-century Perruzzi cut of fifty-eight facets, reworked it, improved on it in an amazing way. I—I envy him and respect him, Mr. Laird. There is no way I could allow his daughter to come to harm."

He meant it. Suddenly Laird felt a small, growing glow of hope. Maybe there was a way out, a chance—but it all depended on this frail, middle-aged, very nervous man.

"How is Katie?" He made it an acceptance.

"About the same as you, Mr. Laird." Meihan shivered and looked around. "Perhaps a little warmer. Tell me—because Stassen may ask me. When her father examined the London diamonds, what did he say about the work I had done?"

"That he hadn't seen better faking."

Meihan was pleased, and showed it. But Laird saw he had to push him on.

"When did you start working for Stassen?"

"In the spring of this year." Meihan looked down at his feet, embarrassed. "I was in Hong Kong; there were certain difficulties with some Chinese about the way I had—well—improved a few diamonds. Stassen offered me a deal; he got me out and brought me here; he supplied the laser equipment I needed—"

Laird stopped him. The guard was coming over. Laird scowled at the man and sat deliberately on the sacking. Grinning, the guard turned away again.

"How much do you know about what is going on?"

Meihan winced. "I have only done my work—"

"That's not what I asked."

"I—I have heard a little." The words came reluctantly.

"Like drugs for diamonds, diamonds for guns?" suggested Laird softly. "Come on, Meihan. How does it work?"

Meihan still hesitated. "After this, I would like a chance to live a little longer."

Laird nodded. "You come with us when we leave."

"All this began with Elsa Manton, not Stassen." The man took another of those quick, nervous glances over his shoulder. "Her late husband handled various secret deals for some Middle East politicals —until things went wrong and they fled to Switzerland. They chose Lugano because Stassen was here and they knew him."

Now that he'd started, Meihan kept going in a quick, whispered torrent of words that seemed to hiss round the old stone walls of the ice-house. After her husband died, Elsa Manton patched up her differences with their previous contacts. They had switched their interests to Africa, they were in the market for military equipment, and Paul Stassen, the ex-mercenary, could supply.

"But there was a problem, Mr. Laird. These people are like many of their kind—they use heroin as their currency." Meihan shrugged. "Arms dealers are cautious; they don't like handling drugs. Even cash money doesn't always attract them; gold can be dangerously bulky."

"Which leaves diamonds?"

"Exactly. A man can carry a king's ransom in his pockets."

So Stassen had set things up. Landed by fishing boat along the Adriatic coast, the heroin came north to Luino on the Swiss border aboard the ubiquitous market trading vans. Stassen collected, took the heroin out through Switzerland to France, then Holland. The Amsterdam narcotics wholesalers paid in diamonds; the diamonds went to the arms agents.

Listening to the whispering voice, watching the guard outside, Andrew Laird could guess at the complexity of the operation. Risks and running costs must be high; the rewards had to be even higher —and being an accepted part of a frontier community was Paul Stassen's biggest asset. But there was one question he had to ask.

"How many arms shipments has Stassen sent them?"

"I'm not sure. There have been a few, much smaller, most before

I arrived." Meihan shook his head. "This one is very big, the one that really matters.

"But even before Elsa Manton had brought Stassen his largest-ever order and her idea of using the Ticino's relief fund convoy as cover, Stassen had hit on an idea of his own. He knew most narcotics wholesalers 'cut' the purity of their heroin supplies as a matter of routine before selling to the streets. He could do the same with diamonds.

"The Amsterdam wholesalers began including parcels of reject stones in their payments. His new recruit from Hong Kong used his laser skills. A percentage of low-value fakes began to be part of each instalment of diamonds received by the munitions suppliers."

"Suppose they find out?" Laird watched the guard carefully. The man had tossed away the stub of his cigarette, was showing the first signs of impatience. "They will, eventually—won't they?"

"Perhaps." Meihan twisted a wan smile. "But it could be a long time, years, before they decide to sell the stones. Even then, there are very few people like your Miguel Holly around—and I had an incentive to work well."

"Money."

"Money—and my life." Meihan gave a small, sad gesture. "Stassen will make an extra three million dollars on this shipment—I would have been given ten per cent."

"Hard luck," said Laird without sympathy. "All right, what about now? How many people does Stassen have on tap?"

"About a dozen here, a few more at the Casino Rosa, the others waiting in Lugano. They'll all be at the Villa tomorrow, to move the trucks."

"What's the position with Stassen?"

"Last night's visitors were his Amsterdam contacts. They paid in diamonds for a new heroin delivery and flew out this morning." Meihan scratched his chin with the diamond thumbnail. "Tonight, if all goes well, Stassen will be in Lugano. He and the Manton woman have to meet the arms dealers and pay a final instalment. Then—I don't know. He may stay with her; he may come back here."

"So you'll get us out tonight?"

"Once Stassen has gone." Meihan moistened his lips. "I—I will come for you first. I can't help the girl on my own." He paused hopefully. "She says you know a way through to the Casino Rosa. If we can get there, to the customs post or—"

Laird stopped him with a quick, warning frown. The guard's patience had ended, and he was coming over. A moment later he stuck his head in the doorway.

"Finished, Signor Meihan?" he asked in a bored voice.

"*Grazie.*" Meihan nodded quickly. He feigned an irate sniff in Laird's direction. "The fool is being difficult. But I'll be back."

The guard grinned with no particular respect. He waited until Meihan had backed out into the daylight. Then the door slammed shut; the lock gave its familiar, heavy click.

If time had seemed to crawl earlier, it became ten times worse now for Laird—but for a very different reason. Could Meihan do it, or would the frail-looking, nervous South African change his mind, be afraid to go through with what he'd promised?

There was nothing Laird could do but wait and wonder, try to occupy his mind with the new information he'd gained, consider the puzzles that were left, then consider them again.

The gaps round the edge of the door told him when it was dusk outside. He heard voices soon after that, and the door opened briefly as his evening meal was delivered. It amounted to a mug of soup and another cold sausage.

Laird made them last, then waited again while the chill of another night began soaking in through the stone walls. It was easy to torment himself, to decide that, after all, nothing was going to happen.

When it did, he was taken by surprise. The first thing he heard was an urgent scraping on the ice-house door, then a barely heard, repeated whisper.

"The light, Laird. Put out the light."

He got over to the switch, flicked it off, and stood in the inky blackness. The lock clicked, the door opened slowly, and Johan Meihan beckoned.

The night sky was heavy with cloud, and a steady drizzle of rain was falling. Lights showed behind most of the Villa Alton's windows; a radio was playing somewhere near. He turned to Meihan.

The man was wearing a dark waterproof coat and held something long and heavy-looking in his left hand.

"Thanks," whispered Laird.

"I had to wait till Stassen left." Meihan made a shaky attempt at a grin. "I'm not very good at this. What do we do with him?"

He pointed. A huddled figure lay motionless on the other side of the courtyard. Going over, Laird knelt and peered at the unconscious guard. Blood was dribbling from a wound in his head. He checked the man's pulse.

"What did you hit him with?"

Meihan showed him what he was carrying. It was an iron fireside poker with an ornate brass handle.

"Is he dead?" he asked.

"No." But it was going to be a long time before this one came round. Laird picked up the long-barrelled revolver lying beside the man, tucked it into his waistband, then signalled to Meihan. "Lend a hand."

They dragged the guard over the damp cobbles, dumped him inside the ice-house, then closed and locked the door. Laird pocketed the key.

"All right, let's get Katie," he said softly. "Where do we go?"

"That way." Meihan pointed to their left. "The rear of the garage block. There's a watchman's office, stairs beside it—she's in the storeroom at the top of the stairs." He made an anxious grab at Laird's arm, stopping him. "But they've got two men on night duty, to keep an eye on the trucks."

"Can you show me?"

Meihan nodded.

They set off, moving quietly through the drizzle, keeping to the shadows, the lights of the villa above them. Meihan stopped Laird at the end of the building. Beyond the corner, a stone's throw distance away, the garage block was a low silhouette backed by the high hedge which hid Paul Stassen's waiting trucks.

Licking his lips, Meihan signalled them on again. Hurrying across the open ground, they reached the other building, then hugging the wall worked round to the far side. Light spilled from an open door, and there was a window beside it. Mouthing to Meihan to stay where he was, Laird crept forward, reached the window, and heard voices. Inching nearer, he risked a quick glance, then pulled back and cursed under his breath.

The layout was as Meihan had described, including a wooden stairway. But there were three men, not two, in the watchman's office—and one of them was Danny Terras. He was sitting on the edge of a table, a can of beer in one hand, grinning at a story one of the guards was telling.

Suddenly the voices were louder. Two figures appeared at the open doorway, and Laird pressed back against the stonework, dropping a hand to the gun at his waistband.

The men came out. One was Terras, turning up the collar of his parka jacket to ward off some of the drizzle. The other was a guard, a shotgun tucked under his arm. They parted, the guard ambling down towards the hedge and disappearing, Terras taking a few steps, then pausing to light a cigarette.

Laird froze, his mouth dry. If Terras came his way, if Stassen's lieutenant was going round to check on the man left to guard the ice-house—his hand tightened on the revolver. That was all it would take; every hope he had would be dashed.

Terras moved off, but in the other direction, towards the front of the villa. Taking a deep, relieved breath, Laird worked his way back to Johan Meihan.

"I saw." Meihan licked his lips. "I thought—"

"It didn't happen." Laird almost smiled at the way Meihan was clutching the old iron poker, wondered if the man knew the way it was shaking. But something else mattered more. "Why didn't Terras go with Stassen this time?"

"Because of tomorrow. Stassen wanted someone in charge here who could make decisions." Meihan grimaced. "He took Lucci instead."

"How long till the man who went to the trucks gets back?"

Meihan shook his head. "Usually he just takes a walk around—a few minutes, no more."

"We need to take both of them." Laird considered Meihan carefully. "I want you to walk in that door. Tell the man you came out for a breath of air, that you think you've seen someone prowling. Get him to that door to take a look."

Meihan hesitated. "There's a telephone. Suppose he—"

"Don't let him use it. Say you're not certain about anything, that you don't want to make him look a fool." Laird paused. "Think you can do it?"

Meihan gave a long sigh, then nodded.

"Now?" he asked.

"Yes." Laird had to grab him as he started. "But put down that damned poker."

Reluctantly Meihan laid it down, swallowed hard, then set off with a reasonably firm stride. Laird gave him a start of a few paces, followed, but kept close to the wall. He had the revolver drawn and ready.

Reaching the door, squaring his shoulders as he stepped into the light, Meihan went in. As his footsteps sounded on the concrete floor, a startled exclamation came from inside. Then Laird heard a murmur of conversation followed by a laugh and the sound of a chair being scraped back. Flattened against the side of the doorway, he waited.

Meihan came out first, stopped, and turned as the guard emerged. The man was grinning and had a thumb hooked above the holstered pistol at his waist.

Taking one step forward, Laird clubbed him hard behind the ear with the revolver, caught him as he slumped, and dragged him back inside with Meihan following.

"No, leave it." He stopped Meihan from closing the door. "Get something to tie him with—and a gag."

Dumping the man down, Laird looked around. The main garage area was in darkness and littered with empty crates. The only vehicle he could see was a small truck lying with its engine partly dismantled. He glanced at the wooden stairway, so temptingly near, and could see the closed door at the top.

Meihan came back. He was carrying a coil of copper wire and some old rags. Moving quickly, they bound and gagged the luckless guard, then dragged him over behind a workbench, out of sight. Panting a little, Meihan beamed his relief and nodded towards the stairway.

"Why don't we just get her and get out?" he suggested.

"This one's friend will be back. We need more time." Laird

handed him the automatic from their captive's holster. "Can you use this?"

Meihan peered awkwardly at the gun, looked worried, but nodded.

"Watch the door."

He went up the wooden stairway two steps at a time, reached the door at the top, saw the key was in the lock, and turned it. When he pushed open the door, Katie Holly was sitting on a wooden box in the middle of the little storeroom, staring at him in near disbelief.

"He meant it." She got up quickly, her expression changing. "He —so he really meant it!"

Then she was beside him, hugging him under the glare of the overhead light. Apart from the box she'd been sitting on, the only other item in the windowless storeroom was an old mattress partly covered by a blanket.

"He's down below, waiting." Still holding her close, Laird heard her give what sounded like a sob. "It's all right—"

"All right?" The muffled noise became a choked laugh. She stood back, her face grimy, her hair uncombed. He saw she'd tried to repair her torn dress with string. Her eyes bright and moist, she shook her head. "I just couldn't believe it would happen."

"We're not clear yet." Laird took her by the hand and out of the storeroom. Closing the door behind them, he told her, "We're waiting for one of your little friends to come back."

They went down the stairs. Katie gave Johan Meihan a hug which left him flushed with embarrassment, then Laird had her get down behind the work-bench where their first captive was already concealed.

"Your turn again." Laird gave Meihan a friendly tap on the arm. "When he comes back, we need someone sitting in that office. Agreed?"

Meihan gave a resigned nod, then looked at the automatic he was still holding.

"These things usually have a safety catch, don't they?" he asked, puzzled.

Laird looked, winced, and nodded. The safety catch was still on. He showed Meihan what to do, then gestured towards the office.

"Just sit, wait, do nothing, and have a smile ready."

Meihan grunted. He seemed to be gradually settling into his new role.

"I'd smile best if Stassen or that damn Manton woman were first in," he said. "Maybe I owed them favours after Hong Kong but not now."

"Then who helped her with her diamond painting—the one with the butterfly inclusion?" asked Laird dryly.

"That?" The reminder opened a wound. "The stone was in one of the Amsterdam parcels. It was so unusual I photographed it, then was fool enough to show her the print." Meihan's mouth trembled angrily. "She took it from me. Her damned abstract painting is a cheap chocolate-box copy."

He turned quickly, walked over to the little office, and sat down stiffly at the table.

Two minutes later the man who had been out patrolling the parked trucks walked back in, his shotgun still under one arm. He saw Meihan, blinked, then came forward, brushing the wet from his shoulders.

"Buona sera, Signor Meihan," he began casually.

The greeting stopped there as Laird stepped out from behind the door, jammed the muzzle of his revolver against the man's ear, and let the hammer click back.

They took the shotgun; then Katie helped herself to the heavy jacket he was wearing before they tied and gagged the man and dumped him beside his friend.

As they finished, the telephone rang in the office. Katie swore softly, Meihan glanced indecisively at Laird.

"From the Villa?" asked Laird as the ringing kept on.

"An extension line." Meihan paled. "But—"

"Leave it." He waited, and after a moment the telephone became silent. With luck, whoever had been at the other end would wait a couple of minutes, then try again. "Time to get out. There's a stream somewhere near—it runs towards the casino pier. Do you know it?"

Meihan nodded. "Back the way we came, beyond the ice-house. Why?"

"Just trust us," Katie told him, fastening her newly acquired jacket. "It's our turn." She glanced at the guard's shotgun, then at Laird. "Mine?"

He shook his head. They had the two hand guns; the thing they really needed was speed.

The drizzle outside had become a steady downpour. They hurried through it, letting Meihan take the lead, reached the cobbled court-yard, and were past the ice-house when a shout came from behind them. A torch beam lanced through the darkness, caught them, steadied, and a shot rang out. The bullet sliced twigs from a patch of bushes close beside them. There was a second shot as they began running and reached the cover of the bushes.

Johan Meihan yelped, staggered, then fell. As Laird and Katie reached him, he made a desperate effort to scramble up again.

"It's my shoulder." He gave a sob of pain as they helped him to his feet. His left arm hung limp, and he would have fallen again if Laird hadn't grabbed him. "Where are they?"

Laird glanced back. There were other lights outside the Villa Alton, some beginning to come their way through the rain, and he thought he recognised Danny Terras's voice shouting orders.

"Getting near." He grabbed Meihan's good arm. "Which way now?"

Meihan swayed and gave him a dazed look. "My gun, I've lost it."

"Johan." Katie made it a plea. "The stream—which way? We'll help you."

"I"—he shook his head as if to clear it—"to your right. Through some trees."

She looked at Laird.

He nodded and they set off again—Katie leading, Laird close behind, half supporting Meihan. The downpour continued; they crashed through half-seen scrub; branches clawed at them in the darkness. Several times Meihan staggered and almost fell, but the voices behind seemed to be fading; there was only the distant glint of a torch.

They reached the trees. Panting for breath, Katie Holly slowed, stopped till they caught up, then turned an anxious, rain-soaked face towards Laird.

"Listen," she said simply.

Laird heard it himself: a steady roar of rushing, tumbling water.

They went on a few yards, then stopped where the ground fell away. The stream was below them, but not the feeble trickle they'd seen at the casino pier exit pipe. The rain was coming down from the hills; the water below was a foaming, angry torrent.

But it was their only way out.

He lowered Meihan to the ground at the top of the slope. The man collapsed and lay still, totally exhausted. Laird turned to Katie.

"Stay with him. I'll see how bad it is."

She nodded. Laird could see by her face that they were sharing the same thought. If the stream was so swollen in the open, what would it be like in the underground stretch nearer the lake?

Tight-lipped, he slithered his way down the steep incline of grass and mud to reach the rushing water, then waded in. The chill hit him like a hammer-blow; the torrent almost swept him off balance for a moment. He could feel loose stones and gravel underfoot shifting with every step he took. But it could have been worse. In mid-stream, the icy, foaming flow still only reached mid-way up his thighs.

He waded a few more steps downstream to make sure, turned, battled back against the spate, and made his way towards the bank. Katie was standing halfway down the slope, but she didn't move to help him. Then Laird saw why and almost groaned. Another figure was behind her in the rain, a figure with a machine-pistol.

"Keep coming, Laird," Danny Terras's voice mocked in the darkness. The man shifted a half-pace, Laird could just make out the wolfish grin on his narrow face and the motionless shape of Meihan lying behind him. "That gun. Get rid of it."

"Go to hell," said Laird wearily, took the revolver from his waistband, and dropped it into the stream.

Terras laughed hoarsely. The machine-pistol swung at Katie as she glanced round, then trained back on Laird again.

"I'd a hunch you might try this way." Terras shifted again slightly. "Your choice, Laird. Out—or I kill you right where you are."

Slowly, resignedly, Laird splashed his way out and reached the start of the muddy ground. He looked up at Terras, saw the murderous glint in his narrowed eyes, and knew it hadn't mattered.

"That's right," said Terras softly. The machine-pistol came up a fraction.

Something was moving higher up the slope. The move became a heaving twist; then Johan Meihan came rolling down the slippery, rain-soaked incline like a runaway log. Some sense, some sound warned Terras. But he hadn't time. As he started to glance round, Meihan's body arrived, knocked the man's feet from under him, and sent him tumbling. Two rounds from the machine-pistol barked wildly into the night; then the weapon had gone from his grasp and went spinning into the water.

Laird sprang, smashed a blow at Terras's twisted face, and blocked a flailing return punch; then they were grappling, locked together in the mud.

A knee slammed into Laird's stomach and left him gasping. He hung on to his wiry, thrashing opponent, saw Terras's teeth show white as the man tried to bite, jerked clear, then butted Stassen's lieutenant hard in the face. Terras squealed with pain; they rolled again, and suddenly they were in the stream.

The first shock separated them as they went under. Laird rose first, saw Terras's head coming up, and sheer instinct took over.

Pistoning with his opened left hand, he forced Terras's head back under and held it there. Almost simultaneously he swung his right arm beneath the man's thrashing knees, lifted them clear of the water, and heaved backwards. Laird felt the man give one spasmodic kick. Then the legs went limp. Laird had been dragged down again; he was struggling free from the man's sagging weight.

Laird got to his feet. He saw something half-submerged that might have been Danny Terras being swept downstream. Then it had gone in the night.

Staggering over, he collapsed half out of the water. Then Katie Holly was with him, pulling, dragging him out, murmuring encouragement, holding him against her. Gasping, he grinned at her, saw Johan Meihan sitting beside them, and nodded gratefully. His sodden clothes clung to him, his body ached from some of Terras's blows—but he felt better with every breath.

"Get me up." He was glad of her support as he hauled himself to his feet. Still panting, he let go, looked at them both, and saw the unspoken bewilderment in their eyes. He shook his head. "We haven't time. Not now."

Katie nodded, understanding, then bit her lip.

"He just appeared—" She stopped it there and gave a helpless gesture.

Laird drew another deep breath and looked around. Nothing moved. He could only hear the rushing water and his own laboured breathing. But the shots from Terras's machine-pistol must have been heard; more of the men from the villa could be heading their way.

"Ready?" he asked.

They nodded. He took another look around, but in his mind's eye he was reliving those frantic few seconds in the water, the moment when Danny Terras's body had been swept away.

It was simple, it was basic; it was something from his days as a first-year medical student, told as a casual, macabre curiosity in a forensic studies lecture.

How to drown someone the easy way. Preferably in a bath—a Victorian murderer, George Joseph Smith, had conveniently disposed of several brides that way until a forensic expert named Spilsbury stumbled on the truth.

Andrew Laird swallowed hard. It had happened, exactly as described in the dry language of that almost forgotten lecture room:

"A sudden rush of water passing up the nasal passages during an act of forced, accelerated immersion can result in an immediate loss of consciousness, particularly if the legs are brought above the victim's head. Without immediate relief, the result is death by drowning."

He came back to what mattered, helped Meihan to his feet, supported him down to the edge of the stream where Katie was waiting, and they waded in together.

The spate of water was still rising, reached almost to Katie's waist, numbing cold. But it was their best chance, their only real chance. Occasionally, though he was trying hard, Johan Meihan gave a low moan as the pain from his wound stabbed through him. Once Katie lost her balance, disappeared, and rose again cursing with low, unbelievable fluency. For Laird, it became an automatic process of moving one leg, then the other.

But there was a low rise of ground ahead, a glow of light beyond it that had to be the Casino Rosa. They waded on, saw the stream headed straight towards a dark patch, where it seemed to disappear, and started for it with a new-found energy.

A metallic click, just audible above the sounds of the water, was their first warning. Then dark shapes appeared on both banks, some kneeling, others moving in a quick, low crouch through the rain. A stray shaft of moonlight escaped through the broken cloud overhead and glinted on weapons.

"*Allora* . . . what have we got here?" said a soft, startled voice. A shaded torch flicked on; the beam swept them carefully. Laird heard a low cry of recognition; then one of the figures was splashing towards them.

"We came looking for you, Mr. Laird," said Willi Dortman with a grin of relief. Face blackened, wearing camouflage overalls, the G.S.G. 9 man gestured to the other figures to help them, then slapped Laird hard on the back. "*Wunderbar.* But did you have to go paddling on a night like this?"

Dortman took over. More men appeared out of the darkness, big men, most of them in the same camouflage overalls, with blackened faces, heavily armed, but surprisingly gentle. Along with Katie and Meihan, Laird was almost lifted out of the stream. Two of the men, one holding a torch, the other producing a first-aid kit, got to work on Meihan's wound. Another two, grinning, wrapped Katie in a waterproof and whisked her out of sight, murmuring apologetically in Italian.

"Here." Dortman gestured Laird down under the shelter of a bush, then squatted beside him. He produced a flask, unscrewed the top, and rammed the flask into Laird's hands. "Try this."

The first mouthful of raw brandy caught at Laird's throat. He gasped, took another glad swallow, and felt the warmth seep down into his body.

"Now." Dortman sat back on his heels. "It was Stassen?"

Laird nodded.

"You know why?"

"Gun-running." Laird used the flask again and wiped his mouth. "They're shipping tomorrow."

"Thank you." Dortman showed no surprise. He turned. *"Maggoire—"*

One of the figures trotted over and squatted beside them.

"Major Galiani, *Brigata Alpina,*" introduced Dortman and winked at Laird. "All he has done so far is complain about his feet getting wet."

The Italian, a short, bulky man with a face ferociously streaked with camouflage cream, grinned at them. His overalls had green collar-patches and a light infantry bugle badge.

"Buona sera, Signor Laird." He glanced at Dortman. "Green light, Willi?"

"Green light," agreed Dortman. "Like to tell your other friends?"

"If the damn radio is still working." Galiani got to his feet and trotted away.

"He knows what he's doing," said Dortman absently, taking back the flask and having a quick gulp at what was left. "Everything's covered. I've got Galiani's squad here; there's a gang of Carabinieri camped on the road beyond the villa. But we were going to have to go gently."

"Till you knew about us?"

"One way or another." Dortman nodded.

"How—?" began Laird.

"You and the diamond lady vanished; you hadn't damn well told me about Bernardo Garri." Dortman scowled at him. "Thank Jo-Jo I heard about that. Even then, I wouldn't have made myself popular with the Swiss without proof." He shrugged. "But this is Italy; they're in NATO, friends. You were heading for the tunnel?"

Laird nodded, still bewildered.

"We came in that way." Dortman was enjoying himself. "But don't worry about the casino—about half the Italian police force are playing the tables there tonight, on expenses. Some of the women with them—" He pursed his lips appreciatively. "You know Stassen is in Lugano?"

"Paying off his suppliers." Laird nodded.

"In diamonds?" Dortman sighed. "Well, if he tries to telephone home, the lines are out of order." The Italian major was striding past in the downpour, a Beretta carbine in one hand, the tubular metal butt still folded back, more of his Alpini moving silently around him. Dortman paused at the sight, then glanced at Laird. "Your diamond lady and your other friend are in good hands. Feel like a walk?"

Laird got to his feet and they set off.

Italy's elite mountain troops, the *Brigata Alpina* develop their special skills for the high country. But Galiani's men showed they were equally effective on lower ground.

Flitting through the night like ghosts, merging with every patch of cover, never hurrying, they still weren't easy to keep up with. They met a first brief pocket of resistance with the Villa Alton already in sight, silenced it with a single burst of automatic fire, then swept on in the rain.

Laird heard the nerve-jamming blast of a stun grenade to his right, then more shots. Two longer bursts from automatic weapons raked the night to his left; then a man was screaming, and two others stood with their hands held high.

It was over. A few isolated shots from the far side of the villa told them that the Carabinieri had arrived. The last spasm of violence was in the kitchen, where Stassen's fat housekeeper tried to knife an Alpini sergeant.

The Alpini infantrymen seemed disappointed that things had finished. Eight prisoners were lined up, some bleeding. Three of their companions were dead; two of the Carabinieri had slight wounds; an Alpini corporal sat cursing a twisted ankle.

Laird helped bandage some of the wounded. Then, while a guard was placed on the trucks and Dortman led a search of the villa, he took the chance to acquire some dry clothes and a coat.

At last, he went back into the rain with Dortman, and they went over to the lines of trucks parked under camouflage netting. Looking at the white paintwork and the Ticino badges, Dortman swore softly.

"It could have worked," he admitted.

"It almost did," said Laird.

The Alpini had forced open a few of the locked containers. But there had also been lists among the papers in Paul Stassen's study.

They walked from truck to truck, Dortman flashing a torch where the doors had been opened. The Alpini had prized the lids off a few of the crates and boxes; the stencils on others told their own story. American M-60 machine-guns were packed beside French grenades and British mortars. One container bulged with German-made Heckler and Koch pistols and ammunition. There were saucer-shaped land mines, compact, wire-guided anti-tank missiles, and heat-seeking rockets.

Yet it was still only a sample.

"How does it feel to have spoiled someone's war?" asked Dortman dryly.

Laird shrugged. There had been other things among Paul Stassen's papers. They had the name of the second ship and details of two East African ports. A team of Carabinieri officers was still working through the rest, gleaning an occasional name or initials and telephone numbers, assembling what looked like becoming a complete list of Stassen's narcotics buyers and his underworld arms sellers.

There was only one area which remained blank. Once the weapons reached East Africa, there was no pointer to their final destination or who was intended to use them, nothing to even hint at the shadow-like people who had hired him.

There were politicians in several places who would claim that gap mattered more than anything. But Laird had something more immediate, more personal on his mind.

"You knew." He eyed Dortman grimly. "You knew it was gun-running. You could have warned me."

"My friend, I only knew it might be." Dortman wiped some of the trickles of rain from his face and scowled defensively. "I also had orders to keep my mouth shut. Interpol had heard whispers but no names; so had NATO Security. There was a buyer in the market, diamonds were involved—are you always told how people know things?" He thumbed savagely towards the trucks. "Trace that stuff back, and half of it was probably stolen from NATO military bases."

"But you came to Lugano."

"I was sent—there's a difference." Dortman sighed. "We're the same kind, Laird. Other people lift us up, put us down. We get on with it from there."

They looked at each other for a moment, then exchanged a wry smile. It was exactly that way.

"There's still Stassen," said Laird.

"Stassen and the woman." Dortman nodded. "My friend, I am about to perform a small miracle—two, if you are cynical. First the Villa telephone will be reconnected. Second someone a lot more important than me will talk to the police in Lugano." He chuckled to himself. "The Swiss are going to be very angry. I may even enjoy it."

Dortman made his telephone calls. It gave Laird a chance to speak to Katie Holly and Meihan. The dead, the wounded, and the prisoners were being cleared from the Villa Alton, but Meihan was being loaded aboard a private ambulance and Katie was going with him on the long road journey round the lake, to Swiss territory and Lugano. The Swiss would want to talk to Meihan; the Italian authorities would want him again afterwards—but for the moment it was a diplomatic move, and the ambulance driver would be in no hurry.

Meihan seemed happily content just to be alive. He watched, smiling as Laird finally helped Katie aboard. Then the doors closed and the ambulance purred away.

The rain eased, then died away at midnight. But the casino pier was still glistening wet when a small, fast police launch flying the Swiss flag arrived a little later. The launch touched briefly, just long enough for Laird and Willi Dortman to get aboard, then swung out again and raced back in a cloud of spray towards the lights of Lugano.

They came in at a landing stage on the north side of the town. A police car was waiting, and the Swiss officers gave a flurry of salutes as a tall man in a black tie and dinner jacket emerged from a second car and came over.

"Top brass," murmured Dortman. "I know him by sight—Eduard Raynard, one of their deputy chiefs. Dragged out of something and doesn't like any of it."

The introductions were brief; Raynard's attitude was chilly.

"We're doing everything that was asked." He frowned at them both, "But Inspector Dortman—and you, Signor Laird—you should understand that Switzerland strongly dislikes your styles of unauthorised investigation."

"But in the circumstances—" murmured Dortman.

"I accept that." Raynard's mouth tightened. "The situation will be discussed later. This man Stassen and Signora Manton are both under arrest. The holding charges are Swiss—complicity in the murder at Zürich and in the fire attack on Signor Garri's shop here in Lugano." He shrugged. "The rest can follow."

"Where did you get them?" asked Laird.

"At the airstrip." Fingering his black tie, Raynard sighed a little. "There were some minor difficulties."

Dortman raised a polite eyebrow. "What kind?"

"The air taxi with their visitors had taken off—it lands at Zürich; they'll be collected there. Stassen and the woman gave no trouble, but their driver—"

"Lucci?" prompted Laird.

"Lucci." Raynard nodded a chill thanks. "He attempted to escape. He was armed. He was—ah—shot dead. Did he matter?"

Dortman shook his head.

"Good." The man showed a slight relief. "I've had a search made of the Manton woman's house—as requested. I understand there's also a request that we let you talk to both of them?"

Dortman nodded. "It could matter."

"The other car will take you." Raynard stopped and drew a deep breath. "This happens to be my wedding anniversary. My wife and I were giving a small party for friends when I was told what was happening."

"I'm sorry," said Laird. "Bad luck."

"Bad luck is an understatement, Signor Laird. My wife is vice-president of the Relief Fund Ladies' Committee."

Spinning on his heel, the deputy police chief stalked back to his car.

It was a short drive through Lugano to the police station. They were met by a pudgy, dark-haired detective inspector named Bianchi, who greeted them with a friendly interest.

"Who do you want to see first?" he asked. "The man?"

"Yes." Dortman stopped him. "Any luck at Elsa Manton's house?"

Bianchi shook his head. "Not a lot—and my boys are good." He beckoned them to his desk. "But she had a safe. This was in it. *Permette* . . ."

The chamois leather pouch was held closed by a drawstring. Opening it, Bianchi casually tilted the pouch, and a small cascade of diamonds rattled out over the desktop.

"They're counted," he said dryly, shovelling them back again. "A nice little nest-egg, eh?"

He took them along to an interview room, and Paul Stassen was brought in after a moment. He didn't have a tie; the laces had been removed from his shoes; his wrists were handcuffed behind his back; his long, coppery hair hung lank across his forehead. But he still eyed them with an insolent defiance as he sat in a chair across the table from them.

"Your turn, Laird," he said sardonically; then, ignoring Bianchi, he frowned at Dortman. "Who's this? Another fearless lawman?"

"Interpol," said Dortman. He got up, walked casually around the man then sat down again. "No curiosity, no questions from you, Mr. Stassen?"

"Not from me." Stassen's face hardened. "And you won't get answers—I'll talk to my lawyers, no one else."

"You'll be wasting your money," said Laird.

"Maybe—maybe not. I'll wait and see." Something like a grin crossed his lips. "I can stir some hellish legal tangles."

Dortman shrugged. "One question, Stassen. It can't make much difference to you. Who were buying those weapons?"

Stassen looked at him for a long moment, then very slowly got to his feet. "No way," he said softly. "I'm in no hurry to be dead."

He was taken out.

"Bianchi?" Dortman glanced quizzically at the Swiss policeman.

"*Sì.*" Bianchi grimaced. "That's how he is."

"And the woman?"

"The same. Maybe for different reasons." Bianchi clasped his hands together and frowned at them, cracking his knuckles. "There is less against her; the courts are always easier on a woman. A few years, then—"

"Then she comes back out to her nest-egg." Dortman nodded a glance of agreement towards Laird. "These diamonds belong to her.

How do we prove how she got them? Even your friend Meihan's word wouldn't be enough on its own."

He was right. Laird could almost hear the legal arguments that could be put forward, had met the same kind of tripwire situation in the world of insurance. But then the thin beginning of an idea stirred in his mind.

"I'd like the diamonds here when we see her."

Bianchi raised an eyebrow but didn't object.

A policewoman brought in an equally impassive Elsa Manton. She hadn't been handcuffed, she hadn't a blond hair out of place, and she carefully smoothed a wrinkle from her skirt once she had sat down.

"Well?" She eyed Laird stonily, then looked at the two detectives. "What is it now?"

"An offer for you, Elsa." Dortman used her first name casually. "You're a good-looking woman."

"So?"

"Good-looking—but past the first bloom of youth. It happens to us all." Dortman sucked his teeth. "I wonder how you'll look maybe ten years from now, Elsa."

"That's clever." She said it calmly, but her face had hardened. "Go on."

"We could help. Some charges could be reduced; one or two might be dropped. It wouldn't be too bad."

"If I changed sides?" She almost laughed. "You think I'd give evidence against Paul?"

"That, and some information about the real people behind the whole deal." Dortman nodded. "You wouldn't have to be afraid. Arrangements could be made—adequate arrangements."

"No." She shook her head. "Don't waste your time. I can cope."

Dortman sat back. Quietly Laird took the chamois leather pouch from his pocket, opened it, and let the hoard of diamonds tumble out. They lay between him and the woman, sparkling in the light. He saw the way she stared at them and casually, deliberately, stirred a few with a fingertip.

"Yours, Elsa?" He didn't wait for an answer. "Paul Stassen pays pretty well, doesn't he? Or would you say they were rewards for loyalty?"

She sat very still, tight-lipped.

"Of course, maybe you're wrong." Laird smiled at her. "Let's find out." He glanced at Dortman and Bianchi. "I need some kind of hammer—a gun will do. And something else, heavy and metal."

Puzzled, still silent, Elsa Manton watched as Bianchi left and came back with a small but thick piece of steel plate. Dortman handed over his gun with a slightly embarrassed air—it was a brand-new Heckler and Koch, still showing traces of packing grease.

"Now." Laird said a silent prayer that Miguel Holly had got it right when he'd told the story of his grandfather. He picked up one of the nearest stones, guessing its weight at around three carats. It had the pure blue-white colour of polar ice. "You know what a diamond is, Elsa? The hardest substance known on earth—right? You can use a diamond to drill the strongest metal."

Carefully he placed the stone on the steel plate. Equally carefully he gripped Dortman's automatic by the barrel, took a deep breath, and brought the butt down like a hammer.

The diamond shattered into tiny fragments. Some scattered across the table and fell into Elsa Manton's lap. Face drained of colour, she stared at them in disbelief. He heard a gasp from Bianchi. Dortman sat as if frozen.

"Strange." Laird grinned deliberately at her. "Now how did that happen? I mean, to a real diamond—" He reached for another stone, then stopped. "No, you choose this time, Elsa. Pick one you're certain about."

She didn't move.

"Pick one." He snapped the words brutally.

Moistening her lips, she reached out and touched a diamond slightly smaller than the first, a stone with a faintly yellow tinge.

"Right." Planes and grains, stresses and structures—he'd been lucky the first time. Would it happen again? "Let's see. Maybe this one is for real."

He placed the diamond on the centre of the steel plate, looked at her, smiled, and brought the automatic's butt down hard.

The fragments flew wider this time. One nicked his cheek, and he could feel a thin trickle of blood. Elsa Manton had her hands gripping the edge of the table. They were shaking; she seemed to have aged.

"Two of them—I just can't understand it," mused Laird. "That's the sort of thing I'd expect if Paul had unloaded a bunch of rejects on you—you know, some of the ones Meihan drilled all over with those little laser holes, then filled up."

"Maybe we should ask him," said Dortman.

"I don't think Paul would do that to her," said Laird with mock disapproval. "Treat someone as loyal as Elsa that way? I can't believe it. Let's try again."

He reached for another diamond.

"No." Elsa Manton shook her head slowly, wearily. Her voice was beaten, broken. "This—this deal you talked about. Suppose I agreed —not to going into a witness box, but to everything else?"

"We could arrange things," said Dortman. "Could we suggest that Danny Terras talked before he died? Would he know enough— including who was buying?"

"Yes."

"You'll do it?"

She brushed some of the tiny, glinting fragments from her lap, picked a last few clinging particles away with her fingertips, then looked up.

"Yes."

Bianchi and the policewoman led her out. Drawing a deep breath, Willi Dortman retrieved his automatic and tucked it away.

"These diamonds—" He hesitated uncertainly.

"They're real." Laird gave him a lopsided grin. "At least, as far as I know."

"You tricked her," Dortman said. "My friend, maybe that makes you some kind of a crafty bastard—but I'm glad." He frowned at the stones. "The two you smashed—how much were they worth?"

"I don't want to know," said Laird and meant it.

He managed to catch a few hours of sleep before morning; then the inevitable aftermath began.

The Swiss police wanted statements; the Italians wanted statements. Osgood Morris came screaming on the telephone from London, and that meant long telex messages back to Clanmore. He saw Katie now and again, briefly, as she was put through the same insistent process.

Willi Dortman turned up. Laird escaped with him long enough to visit Bernardo Garri in his hospital bed. Anna was there too, was able to smile, to confirm that Garri was on the mend. He wanted to see Johan Meihan, but Meihan was having some new X-rays taken of his shoulder. All Laird could do was leave a message that he'd be back.

On the return journey to the police station, they skirted the Piazza Riforma. Flags were flying; a brass band was playing; a long, slow convoy of white trucks was driving away.

But there were more officials, more uniforms waiting. Osgood Morris came on the phone again. He sounded happier; the mood everywhere was better.

Elsa Manton was talking, just as she'd agreed.

At last it was finished. It was close to midnight when he left the police station and walked back along the lakeside to the Hotel Orchidea.

Jo-Jo was at the desk. He was playing chess again over the telephone. He murmured a greeting, gave Laird his key, then got back to his game.

Laird went up to his room. The curtains hadn't been closed, and he stood for a spell looking at the bright lights and traffic below, then at the placid, peaceful darkness of the lake beyond them.

It was his last night; he was due to start back to London in the morning. On an impulse he lifted the telephone and asked for Katie's room extension. There was no reply.

Putting down the phone, he tossed his jacket over a chair, threw his tie after it, and decided he might as well get some sleep. He was unbuttoning his shirt when he heard a key turn in the room door. It opened. He heard a soft murmur of thanks; then Katie came in.

She wore a dressing gown; she had a bottle in one hand, two glasses in the other. She grinned at him and set them down.

"I never could drink alone," she said. "How about you?"

"The same." Solemnly he poured wine into the glasses. He saw she was wearing her diamond pendant. "You got it back?"

"Johan had it." She lifted one of the glasses and sipped, watching him over the edge. "He—well, seems to have vanished now."

"That's bad. Has he enough money?"

She nodded.

"To Johan." Laird lifted his glass, drank it, then sat it down. "Any plans for tonight?"

"Maybe." He saw the mischief in her eyes and something more. "But there's one extra thing you'd better know about diamonds. They scratch."

"I'll risk it," said Laird.

She switched off the room light. The dressing gown had gone when she came into his arms.

This story is fiction, but in May 1984 customs officers at the port of Chalcis, in Greece, raided the cargo ship *Athanassious S.* after a tip-off. They found false bulkheads fitted to three large tanker trucks being shipped to North Yemen. They seized 22,000 automatic pistols and two million rounds of ammunition with an estimated value of five million dollars.

The three trucks had been loaded aboard the cargo ship at the Bulgarian port of Burgas. False documents said they were being supplied by a non-existent West German firm; they were being shipped to two named Yemenis who have never been traced.

West European law enforcement agencies agree the pistols and ammunition may have been a small instalment of a much larger quantity of weapons of all kinds being smuggled out aboard trucks being shipped to the Middle East and East Africa.

About the Author

Michael Kirk, a popular and prolific mystery writer, is also a novelist and screenwriter. A native Scot, he lives in Glasgow with his wife and three children.